MIK-SHROK

Gloria Repp

illustrated by Jim Brooks

JOURNEY
F O R T H™

Greenville, South Carolina

Library of Congress Cataloging-in-Publication Data

Repp, Gloria, 1941-
  Mik-Shrok / Gloria Repp ; illustrated by Jim Brooks.
    p.   cm.
  Book one of a three-part fictional history: "Adventures of an
Arctic Missionary".
  Summary: In 1950, at the Eskimo village of Koyalik in the Alaska
Territory, two young missionaries' prayers are answered when they
receive a dog sled-team of huskies with Mik-Shrok as its leader.
  ISBN 1-57924-069-0
  [1. Missionaries—Fiction.   2. Sled dogs—Fiction.   3. Dogs—
Fiction.   4. Alaska—Fiction.   5. Christian life—Fiction.]
I. Title.
PZ7.R296Mi   1998
[Fic]—dc21
                                                          98-8838
                                                            CIP
                                                            AC

Mik-Shrok

Project Editor: Debbie L. Parker
Designed by Duane A. Nichols
Cover and illustrations by Jim Brooks

Grateful acknowledgement for Siberian Husky references to Bill and
Harriet Lawrence of Starfire Kennels, Greenville, SC.

© 1998 Journey Books
Published by Bob Jones University Press
Greenville, South Carolina 29614

ISBN 1-57924-069-0

15   14   13   12   11   10   9   8   7   6   5   4   3

Dedicated to Duke,

my first and best-loved dog

—and to all his loyal tribe

Books by Gloria Repp

The Secret of the Golden Cowrie
The Stolen Years
Night Flight
A Question of Yams
Noodle Soup
Nothing Daunted
Trouble at Silver Pines Inn
Mik-Shrok

Contents

Have not I commanded thee?
Joshua 1:9

1 To Koyalik

Steve Bailey held onto the table with one hand and grabbed for his cup with the other. The boat tilted even farther, tipping the small room on end, then slowly righted itself.

He glanced at his wife, Liz, who sat across the table beside two members of the crew. She had turned white, and Steve knew she was feeling sick again. But when he raised an eyebrow at her—*How're you doing?*—she sent him a quick smile.

The captain stepped into the small galley and stood with his feet planted wide apart, his rubber slicker streaming with rain. "Bad storm." He raised his voice above the roaring outside. "It's going to really bite us in the face tonight. Hope I can get you to Koyalik before then."

Steve left the table to make space for the captain and stepped to the open doorway of the galley. He leaned out, but not too far. Rain mixed with snow pelted sideways across the tiny deck. Torrents of ocean spray slashed at the oil drums and crates of supplies. Just beyond rose the dark, heavy swells of the Bering Sea.

Somewhere across all that water lay Koyalik.

Was it only yesterday that they'd left Chicago to come to Alaska? Ever since they'd landed at the Nome airport and found no one to meet them, the minutes had seemed like hours. And each hour had brought more questions.

The boat rose to the top of a long wave and plunged down its other side. Steve braced himself against the door frame. Liz crept up next to him, and he wrapped one arm around her.

The howling wind made normal speech impossible, so he leaned down and shouted into her ear. "Wish we'd stayed in Nome?"

She shook her head and said something back.

He grinned, then tightened his hold on her as the boat lurched down the side of another mountainous wave. Finally he said, "Looks like rain, doesn't it?" She giggled, and they turned back into the galley.

The two crew members had gone to the rear of the boat and were tightening ropes on the cargo. The captain had moved up to the pilothouse to take the wheel. His place at the table had been filled by the first mate, an Eskimo.

The mate seemed to be joking with the Eskimo girl who did the cooking. They spoke in Eskimo, and from the way they laughed, Steve could tell they were all friends.

The girl worked steadily at the stove, filling bowls with thick brown stew. The stove was surrounded by an iron railing, and every time the boat rolled, the pans slid across to bang against the railing, but she didn't seem to mind. She served up biscuits to go with the stew, sliced thick wedges of blueberry pie, and poured coffee without spilling a drop.

When the captain came back to eat, he switched on the radio and listened to the news and weather in grim silence. The report ended with an enthusiastic voice urging all concerned Alaskans to write to Congress in support of statehood.

Steve heard it with interest. "Seems like there's a lot of discussion these days about Alaska becoming a state," he said.

"Discussion?" growled the captain. "Is that what you folks in the Lower Forty-Eight call it? It's a fight, I'll tell you.

Congress thinks Alaska's just a few people rattling around up here in the wilderness. Well, we'll show them! We're fed up with being a colony!"

"Sounds reasonable to me," said Steve. "If you were a state, you'd have your own Congressmen to represent you. Might make a big difference."

"Sure it would. Better not get me started!" The captain finished his pie and leaned back in his chair.

He gazed at Steve with a glimmer of a smile and said, "Been wondering about you two. Aren't tourists, are you?"

Steve smiled. "No, we're missionaries. My wife's a teacher, and I'm a pilot."

"How come you're in such a hurry to get to Koyalik?"

"A friend of ours works with the Eskimos in Koyalik," said Steve. "He's got a small plane there, and he needed some help."

"That would be Pete," said the captain.

"You know him?" asked Steve in surprise.

"There's only two white men in Koyalik, and only one of them flies a plane," said the captain. "So why didn't Pete fly up to Nome and get you?"

"That's what we're wondering," said Steve slowly. "Last we heard from Peter, he was planning to meet us in Nome. A man at the airport said we could fly down to Koyalik with the mail plane. But we didn't want to wait around Nome for two days."

The captain shook his head. "Well, the weather's been good up till now. Something must have happened to him. That's Alaska for you. Had a pilot friend who took off for Fairbanks, and no one ever saw him again."

Steve had thought briefly about a plane crash, then had put it out of his mind.

The boat rolled to one side and back again; Steve caught his plate just as it slid off the table. The captain leaped to his feet, and Steve looked up in alarm, but the man was only getting some more coffee.

"Yep, I knew Pete." The captain took a swallow from his steaming cup and sat down again. "He was a good man."

Steve flinched at the past tense.

The Lord wouldn't let something happen to Peter, would He?

The captain was still talking. "Must have been your stuff I brought down to him a couple weeks ago." He glanced at Liz. "A big trunk and six packing cases—should have known a woman was movin' in."

Liz smiled. "I appreciate your taking care of our supplies," she said politely. "It was quite a challenge trying to decide what to bring."

She was using her teacher's voice, Steve thought, the one she kept for difficult parents.

He decided to change the subject. "So, do you think the storm is going to keep us from going ashore at Koyalik?"

"Maybe," said the captain. "We'll have to see when we get there. In an hour or so."

By the time they had anchored offshore from Koyalik, the wind had eased a little. "We'll put you ashore in the dinghy," said the captain. "There's no dock, y'know. Inshore waters are too shallow for this boat."

The shore must be at least two miles away, Steve thought, but the little boat nosed stubbornly toward it. The waves still looked like mountains of water. They tossed the small dingy high, then swallowed it again a moment later.

He tried to keep his eye on a single light that gleamed through the evening dusk. Every time they went down into the trough of a wave, the light disappeared. Then he found it again as they rose to the peak of the next wave.

Liz huddled beside him in the open boat. Rain dripped off the hood of her jacket and ran down her face like tears, but when Steve pointed to the light, she smiled.

They chugged on and on through the waves until finally the captain cut the motor and one last breaker thrust them onto the sandy beach. Steve took Liz's arm, and they splashed quickly to shore.

The captain tossed their luggage to Steve, then he waved away their thanks. "Good luck," he called. "You'll need it." He pushed off, started the motor again, and left them in the gathering darkness.

"Steve, look!" said Liz in a low voice.

He turned. Behind them stood a dozen red-cheeked Eskimo children. Most of them wore fur-ruffed parkas, and all of them were smiling.

"Hello," Liz said with a smile. "I'm glad to see you. Can you show us where to go?"

No one answered, but the smiles grew broader. Two of the older boys picked up the suitcases. The rest of the children led the way to a two-story log building that overlooked the beach.

This must be the Trading Post, thought Steve. Peter had said he lived in a room at the Trading Post, above the general store, the post office, and the schoolroom. An old trader ran the whole operation. Maybe he'd know something about Peter.

One of the boys opened a wooden door for them, and they stepped into a long, dim, smoke-darkened room. Traps and guns and animal skins hung on the walls. The air smelled of fish, and of potatoes, onions, and apples.

Eskimo men, wearing parkas with the hoods thrown back, sat around a large cast-iron stove. Beyond them, several Eskimo women stood at a wooden counter. A tall white man with a grey beard watched from behind the counter.

Everyone had stopped talking.

2 It's Not Much

Steve glanced at Liz, detoured around a barrel of apples, and headed for the counter. Before he could say anything, the man leaned across the counter, holding out a large, work-hardened hand. "Welcome. I'm Gus Svenson, the trader here." He threw a good-humored glance at the children. "And sometime schoolteacher too."

The women at the counter smiled shyly, and Liz smiled back.

Quickly Steve introduced himself and Liz, explaining why they had come to Koyalik by boat.

"Hmmm." Gus gave him a sharp glance. "We'd better talk. Sit down. Put your jackets there—they'll dry in a bit. You need something hot to drink."

The worry inside Steve coiled a little more tightly. He followed the older man across the room.

One of the Eskimo women brought mugs of black tea, and the men made room around the stove. Steve and Liz sat on blocks of firewood that someone pulled forward, and Gus sat down too, carrying a mug of his own.

"Quite a storm blowing, isn't it?" he said. They talked for a while about the storm and the boat and its captain. Steve waited impatiently.

Liz answered with her usual energy. She even described the blueberry pie, but he could tell that she was as worried as he. The Eskimos listened without saying anything, although they looked as if they understood the conversation.

Warmth seeped into Steve's chilled frame, and he tried to relax.

Finally the old trader put down his mug. "Well, it's a sad story about Peter," he said. "Pete took that plane of his to explore an area up north of here—somewhere over by Totson Mountain, I think. Landed okay on a lake, but then a storm blew up and smashed his plane to smithereens.

Liz made a sound of distress, and the man darted a glance at her. "No, no, he's still alive and kickin'. He was pretty badly injured, trying to keep the plane from sinking to the bottom of the lake, but he managed to call for help on his radio. They got him out all right. Took him to a hospital in Fairbanks. Then yesterday we heard they'd transferred him to some hospital down in Seattle."

Scenes from his own nightmares about crashing spun through Steve's mind. "When did this happen?" he asked. His mouth was so dry he had to take another sip of the bitter tea.

"Just this weekend." Gus rubbed the bald spot on top of his head. "I didn't know you were coming so soon—or that he'd made plans to meet you."

"What about the plane?"

Gus shrugged. "Still at the bottom of the lake, as far as I know. No way to get it out. They'll just leave it there."

He took a long drink of his tea. Then he stood up, slowly unbending his tall, thin body. "Pete had asked if you could stay here for a while. I've got one room upstairs beside his—it's not much . . ."

The room certainly was small, Steve thought. But they would manage. His mind still reeled with the news about Peter, and he had to concentrate hard on looking around.

Besides a cupboard and a sink, there was space for only the bed and the tiny stove. The wooden crates they had sent ahead were stacked against one wall.

Liz sat down on their trunk with a happy sigh. "It's good to see this again."

There was no chair, and no room for their suitcases on the floor, so Steve put them on top of the crates. Liz peered into the bathroom at the far end of the room and came out looking puzzled. "There's no water in the faucets."

Steve had to grin. "Did you see the barrel of water outside our door?"

She groaned. "Okay, so the faucets are just for decoration. And the bathtub is just a big washbasin? Never mind. I'm asleep on my feet. At least we've got a bed, and the floor doesn't move." She yawned. "Where'd we put those sleeping bags?"

The room was cold, but Steve decided not to build a fire. Considering the drafts that he could feel already, the little stove would take too long to warm up the room. They changed hurriedly, shivered over the tiny washbasin, and scrambled into their sleeping bags.

Then they prayed together. Steve thanked the Lord for His care and asked for wisdom in this new situation.

After he finished, Liz said drowsily, "You know what? Peter's letter mentioned someone named Victor, didn't it? Maybe Victor was there tonight. We should have asked."

"You're right. I'll check with Gus in the morning," said Steve.

She fell silent in the icy darkness, and Steve continued to pray silently. He wanted to talk to the Lord about Peter. And about the man named Victor. And about the bright-eyed children and the dark-faced adults. But he could not frame more than a few words without dozing off. He awoke during the night and heard singing. It was wild and sad and lonely, composed of many voices, each with its own mournful tune.

Sounds like wolves, he thought, remembering his boyhood days in Minnesota. I'll have to ask Gus.

He awoke again at dawn. Liz was still asleep, so he dressed quietly and went down a shaky wooden stairway to explore the village.

Where was everyone? He walked past one log cabin after another. The only sounds came from waves breaking on the beach and the sea birds flying overhead. But washing blew on clotheslines, and fish hung in orderly scarlet rows on dooryard racks. Salmon, he thought.

The storm had gone, but the air was cold, and clouds hung low. He paused to look at the river. It curved past the village, widened into a lagoon, and then cut through a sandy headland and emptied into the sea.

That's the beach where we landed last night, he thought. He smiled at the memory of the children's welcome.

Several dozen cabins clustered beside the river and along the beach. Each had a small storehouse, built up on stilts, and each had its own path. The paths joined to form a wide lane that ran past the Trading Post. The landscape seemed strangely wide-open and uncluttered; finally he realized why. There were no trees, no telephone poles, no electric wires.

This is a whole different world, he told himself. But they've got to have an airstrip. It's probably on the edge of town. He wandered past the outlying cabins and found it in the rough tundra grass.

Slowly he paced down the narrow gravel strip, his footsteps crunching as he went. It looked barely long enough to land a plane, but he'd heard that Alaskan runways were short.

He paused beside a 55-gallon drum of aviation gasoline. This was where Peter had fueled his plane.

Until this moment, he hadn't let himself really think about what had happened. But now . . . The tiny airstrip, deserted in the chilly grey light, seemed more dismal than he could bear.

He sat down on the gravel with his back against the metal drum of gasoline.

Okay; I've got to deal with this, he thought. I came here to help Peter with the ministry. To fly the plane. I don't know these people, and they don't know me. I can't even speak their language. Now there's no plane. No ministry?

He put his head in his hands.

Was God shutting the door here? Perhaps they should go back to Chicago and ask the Mission for another field.

A familiar-sounding verse crept into his mind. *Have not I commanded thee?*

He thought back to the day he and Liz had dedicated themselves to go anywhere the Lord should lead. Shortly afterward, they'd heard about a ministry to the Eskimos, and their hearts had leaped to respond.

God had led them step by step through months of preparation, then to the Mission. Finally they'd learned about Peter and the work in Koyalik. It seemed the perfect opportunity to use their skills—Steve as a pilot, Liz as a teacher.

Had God changed His mind?

Steve gazed across the long sweep of golden-brown tundra. *No.*

God doesn't change, he thought. Not His mind. Not His promises. He's brought us here, I know that. Even if there's no airplane, there's still the people. But how will we ever—

He turned his head at a distant rustling sound. An Eskimo boy was walking toward him, followed by a scrawny dog. The boy stopped at the edge of the airstrip and looked at him.

"Hi," said Steve automatically. "How are you?"

The boy said nothing, but he smiled widely enough to show two teeth missing in front. Apparently satisfied that he could stay, he came a few steps closer and stood quietly.

He looked off toward the distant hills, and Steve followed his gaze. The hills curved behind the village like a protective shield. Liz would like their colors—deep red and yellow and brown. She'd be curious, too, about the boy.

Steve jumped to his feet. Liz was probably up by now. He'd go find her, and they could explore the village together. He nodded to the boy and headed for the Trading Post.

The boy followed Steve at a distance, but soon he disappeared.

Liz was dressed and had started arranging their belongings. "I wondered where you went." She glanced up at him. "Oh, something good's happened. You have that look on your face."

She could always tell. He grinned. "I don't know why or how, but—in spite of everything—I'm sure the Lord wants us here. He even gave me a verse."

He picked up his Bible. "Something like 'Haven't I commanded you?' Any idea where it is?"

Liz thought for a minute. "Pastor used it in his message a couple of weeks ago, didn't he? Try Joshua. One of those early chapters."

"Yes, here it is, in chapter one. God was talking to Joshua just before they began fighting for the land."

"Like us, huh?" she said with a smile. "Read it to me."

They read the whole chapter and prayed together. Steve didn't say anything to Liz about the questions that had followed him back to the Trading Post. Where would they live? How would they learn the language? With Peter gone, how would they reach these people?

They put the room in order and went downstairs to see about breakfast.

Gus was in the kitchen, frying pancakes on a big black stove. He piled their plates high, set out cups and a steaming teapot, then leaned against the counter.

"Well, what have you young folks decided to do? No, don't look at me like that, Steve. I saw your faces last night. Bit of a shock, wasn't it, about Peter? I wouldn't blame you if you turned right around and went home." He cocked his head. "The mail plane should come tomorrow, if you're in a hurry."

"We're staying," said Steve. He paused, trying to choose the right words. "We want to get to know the Eskimos; that's the first thing."

The old man's bright eyes studied him. "Well, I'm not much for religion myself, but I liked Peter and the way he did things. These are good people. The best you'll find anywhere."

He stopped to pour canned milk into his coffee, and Steve concentrated on the crisp brown pancakes. Yes, Peter had told them that these were good, hard-working people. But he'd said they had great fears too. They needed Christ.

After a while Steve said, "Peter mentioned someone called Victor Norlik. Do you know where he lives?"

"Yes, but it won't do you much good. He's away at his fish camp. That's where a lot of the people are."

Steve paused with his fork halfway to his mouth. "I went for a walk this morning, and it looked like everyone was sleeping in."

The trader nodded. "They were up late, fishing. Besides, we don't have alarm clocks here."

"Do you have wolves?" asked Steve. "Thought I heard some last night."

Gus shook his head. "No, the wolves mostly keep to the hills. You probably heard the dogs. Each family has its own dog team, and those huskies get to singing at night. They're part wolf, you know."

He picked up their empty plates and dropped them into a dishpan of soapy water.

"Thank you for a wonderful breakfast," said Liz. "We'll help you clean up." She tossed a dishtowel to Steve and began wiping off the counter.

He dried dishes as fast as the old man could wash them, and at the same time he made plans.

First they'd look around the village. Then . . . what about Victor? He spoke English, and they could talk about the work here in Koyalik. He might even be a Christian.

Steve dropped the last fork into the cocoa tin Gus used for a holder.

No matter where that fish camp was, he had to find Victor.

3 Up the River

The village had awakened. One woman sat outside her cabin to work. She wore a green-printed cotton cover over her parka, and her hair was pulled back from her round, handsome face. Next to her was a tub filled with salmon.

Steve and Liz stopped to watch as she used a curved knife to clean the fish in quick, efficient strokes. A young boy hung each fish—flattened, beheaded, and trimmed—on the drying rack.

"What beautiful salmon!" exclaimed Liz.

"Look at that one," said Steve. "It must be three feet long."

The woman smiled but did not reply.

"Is this a good time for fishing?" asked Steve.

The woman said something to the boy, and he answered for her. "Some pick berries." He waved toward the hills. "Old people don't fish."

"Thank you," said Steve, glad that the boy spoke a little English. He motioned toward a woman who sat nearby, working on an animal skin. "Can you tell me what she's doing?"

"She fix a sealskin," the boy said. "After it all sewed up, we put seal oil in it."

He turned to hang another salmon on the rack, and his mother said something to him. He translated with a smile. "My mother say she send a fish and some greens to Trading Post for your dinner."

"Oh! Tell her, 'Thank you very much!' " exclaimed Steve. "It's been a while since I've had fresh salmon."

Liz smiled at the woman, then they walked slowly down the path. "Let's go over to the beach," said Steve. "Then I want to show you the airstrip."

"I'm freezing cold," said Liz. "Remember we were going to buy some heavy jackets when we got here? Maybe Gus will lend me one for today. I'll meet you down at the beach."

She headed back to the Trading Post, and Steve turned toward the beach. All around him, Eskimo men were busy—one cleaning his rifle, another mending a fishnet, another bent over the outboard motor for his boat. The women worked too, and children played everywhere.

Once in a while he caught snatches of conversation, but he couldn't understand a word. Eskimo sounded like a stream of soft, purring sounds interspersed with chuckles, he thought. But his words probably sounded just as strange to them.

He climbed down a rocky slope to the beach and strolled along the sand, stopping to collect a few clamshells. A man pushed a wooden wheelbarrow past him and then parked it near the ocean's edge. He bent to pick up handfuls of something from the shallow water.

Steve drew closer. They were purple-black mussels.

"Are those good to eat?" he asked.

The man answered in English. "Yes. I like better than clams."

Steve smiled and gathered as many as he could without getting his feet wet. He put them in the wheelbarrow.

"Looks like you've got good boots," he said. "Do they keep out the water?"

"Very good. My wife make them. *Oogruk* skin rubbed with seal oil. Better than rubber." He gave Steve a friendly smile.

Maybe this man could help him find Victor, Steve thought. "Perhaps you can tell me—where do people go to fish around here?"

The man waved at the hills behind the village, as the boy had done. "We catch fish in traps. Up the river." He darted in and out of the water, gathering more mussels.

"I'm looking for someone named Victor Norlik," said Steve.

"Yes," the man said. "Yes, I know Victor. He go to his fish camp."

"That's what the trader told me. Do you know if there's any way I could hire someone to take me up there?"

The man shrugged and turned back to picking up mussels. After a while he said, "Maybe that man over there. He need money." He motioned to an older man sitting farther down the beach. Apparently he had nothing to do but gaze at the ocean.

Steve introduced himself to the old man, then explained what he wanted. He paused. "I could pay five dollars if you would take me."

The man sat in silence for a moment. Steve fidgeted. They both watched an Eskimo step into his kayak at the water's edge and paddle smoothly out over the waves.

Perhaps I didn't offer him enough, Steve thought. Gas is expensive here.

"If it's a long way, I could pay you more," he said with a smile. "How about ten dollars?"

The old man stirred, as if from a dream. He got to his feet. "My wife a little bit sick. I think she need me." Slowly he walked down the beach.

The next man Steve asked did not speak English, or else he chose not to understand the question.

Well, this is getting me nowhere, thought Steve. He climbed the rocky headland with long strides and turned toward the Trading Post.

He *had* to find Victor. Sunday was coming up fast. He had no idea whether Peter held a regular church service—or where. It was so hard to talk to these people! He couldn't even get one of them to take him up the river. What was he doing wrong? And what was taking Liz so long?

He found her standing in the general store of the Trading Post, talking to an Eskimo woman. "Oh, Steve, come and meet this dear lady," she said. "Gus brought her to me, and she's going to get us some good, warm parkas. Isn't that wonderful?"

"It sure is," he said. For a few minutes they talked about the cold weather coming, and then Liz took the woman up to their room to show her something.

Steve wandered into the stockroom, where Gus was unpacking a crate of canned goods. "What's the fastest way to learn Eskimo?" he asked abruptly.

Gus gave him a sideways glance. "Good to hear that you want to learn," he said. "Lots of white men depend on an interpreter, but that doesn't always work out very well. And most of the older folk don't speak a word of English."

He stopped to pry open another crate. "What you do is get yourself a notebook and ask a lot of questions. Victor—the man you asked about—translated for Peter and helped him get started."

"I sure do want to get ahold of Victor," said Steve. "I tried to hire someone to take me up the river to his fish camp, but no one wanted to. I thought one of the men would jump at the chance to earn a little cash."

Gus chuckled. "No Eskimo likes to work for another person, especially for money. And they don't like to feel pushed. Never try to hurry an Eskimo. Just ask someone if you can go along sometime, and he'll give you a ride."

He straightened up, rubbing his back. "But you don't want to be taking a trip upriver any time soon. My old bones tell me there's a storm coming."

The big, old-fashioned radio in the Trading Post kitchen confirmed the trader's prediction. That afternoon, wind and pounding rain swept through the village.

After supper, Steve piled more wood into the stove and sat on the trunk to finish his letter to the Mission. He'd waited until now so he could give them the latest information about a church, if there was one. But Gus didn't know anything about a church, and with Victor away, he had nothing more to add.

"Listen to that!" Liz looked up from where she sat on the bed, writing to her family. She tilted her head toward the muffled booming of the ocean. "Those must be huge waves if we can hear them all the way up here."

She bent over her letter again, then paused. "Do you think the Mission will decide to keep on with the work here at Koyalik?"

Steve had been thinking about that. "It doesn't look very promising right now, does it? Two inexperienced missionaries who're new to Alaska and can't even speak the language. They might not let us stay."

"But what did Gus say about something freezing?"

"That's right. There won't be any more boats until spring because of freeze-up. Sounds like it's coming soon." He glanced down at what he had written. "We can't very well fly out and leave our stuff here all winter. I'll put that in my letter."

He didn't tell the Mission that the obstacles to reaching the Eskimos in Koyalik seemed impossibly high. But these people need Christ, he thought. I've got to hang onto that verse the Lord gave us. He's the one who sent us here.

After he'd finished the letter, Steve jumped to his feet. "Gus said that the mail plane usually comes on Mondays and Thursdays. I'm going to take this down to him so it can go out first thing in the morning."

But the wind blew at gale force during the next two days, bringing icy rain and a flurry of wet snowflakes. The weather was too bad for the mail plane to fly in on Thursday, and Steve's letter waited with everything else that the bush pilot would pick up.

Steve and Liz spent their time huddling around the little stove or staring out the rain-streaked window or talking to Gus. Liz helped in the kitchen and persuaded Gus to teach her how to make caribou stew.

Steve made sure he was there whenever the Eskimo men gathered downstairs around the big stove. He listened and asked questions and wrote a few words in his notebook. The words looked strange and incredibly long, and no one knew for sure how to spell them, so Steve consulted with Gus and made up his own spelling system. He watched for the man who had been gathering mussels, but he didn't come in.

Saturday morning, the Eskimo woman brought over the parkas she had found for them. Steve's was short, since he was taller than most Eskimo men. Liz was more slender than most of the women, so hers was too big around. But both jackets were made of warm caribou skins, the fur turned inward, and each hood was trimmed with a ruff of wolverine fur.

She had also brought them each a pair of boots. Gus tapped the soft moosehide bottoms. "*Mukluks*," he said. "Use them only in the snow. They're lined with felt and they'll keep you warmer than anything the white man has ever invented."

The woman would take no money. "We have extra," she said with a broad smile. "You keep warm."

Late that afternoon while Steve stood at the counter talking to Gus, the door of the Trading Post opened. An unfamiliar Eskimo entered, bringing a gust of rain with him. He flung back the hood of his parka and strode across the wooden floor. He was taller than most of the other men, with well-trimmed black hair and sparkling eyes.

"I hear you look for me," he said to Steve. "I am Victor Norlik."

4 Something Caught!

When they told Victor about Peter's accident, the young Eskimo's eyes grew sad. "Peter is good man, very good," he said. "Peter tell me you are coming. He very glad." He brightened. "We glad too."

They learned that Peter usually met with a small group of Eskimos at Victor's house on Sunday mornings.

"You talk to people?" asked Victor, looking doubtful.

"Yes," said Steve, and together they planned a service for Sunday.

Steve would tell them a little about himself, and Victor would translate it into Eskimo. Steve thought the people might be interested to know that Minnesota, where he had grown up, had cold winters much like those in Alaska.

"Do any of them have a Bible?" he asked.

"No," said Victor. "Not read English."

"Maybe I could read some verses and you could translate?"

"May be." Victor pronounced it as two words, Eskimo fashion. "One or two verses. That very hard."

And at the end of the service, perhaps he and Liz could sing a hymn together in English, Steve thought. Even if no one understood the words, they might enjoy the music.

On Sunday morning, they went to Victor's cabin early. Steve had a vague idea of helping to set up chairs. They entered through a small outer room that was crowded with a dog sled, steel traps, an axe, a saw, animal hides, a barrel, stacks of canned goods, and an assortment of boots. Parkas, two pairs of snowshoes, and a tangle of dog harnesses hung on the wall.

Victor's wife, Nida, welcomed them inside the snug, two-room cabin. "Come in, come in," she said with a bright smile. She was a plump, neat woman who spoke English as well as Victor.

When Steve saw the simple furnishings—a table, a few chairs, a pile of caribou skins—he wondered where the people would sit. But he soon stopped wondering.

Later, back at the Trading Post after the service, he said to Liz. "Nine people! That's if you include us and Victor's family."

"You can't count Victor's children," said Liz with a teasing smile. "Those three little boys stayed in the back room the whole time. And you can't count us."

"Well, okay. Four people in church this morning." Steve had to laugh at his own disappointment. "When I preached to my dog team back home, I had a bigger congregation!"

"Maybe it's because they know Peter's gone. They didn't realize what a fine, handsome, *brilliant* young man would be taking his place." Liz got up to hug him.

"Silly girl," Steve said, but he held her tightly. "What did you think about Victor?"

"I don't know what to think. He's certainly friendly, but I'm not sure he's a Christian." She moved to the washbasin and began rinsing out their cups. "I wonder what made him invite us to the whale hunt tomorrow."

"I told him I wanted to follow him around and learn about everything he does," said Steve. "That seemed to surprise him. Guess I'll start by learning about whales."

He fed some more wood to the stove. "Tomorrow could be an exciting day. The mail plane is supposed to come; maybe we'll get some news." With a glance at the empty wood box, he added, "I'd better haul up some more wood, or we'll freeze in here tonight."

After lunch the next day, Victor walked with them down to the beach, where his uncle and a cousin waited. "My uncle's boat," he said. "It has motor and plenty big for us all."

The men stowed guns, harpoons, and a pile of fishnet in the wide, flat bottom of the boat, then they pushed off from the beach. Before long, they were putt-putting over dark green waves. The spray that blew into the boat was icy cold.

"Keep eyes open for seals too," shouted Victor. He stood up to scan the ocean, one hand on his gun.

No one saw a seal, however, and finally he called, "Getting close to net."

A row of charred driftwood floats marked the position of the net, but Steve didn't see them until Victor started counting them aloud.

"Some not show," he said. "Something caught!"

The uncle stood up and put a hand on Victor's arm. "Do not get excited. Stay quiet."

The missing section of floats appeared briefly, then dipped below the water. A huge white shape rose to the surface, turned, and rolled back down out of sight.

"Whale!" cried the young cousin. "Victor, the harpoon!"

"Do not get excited," shouted the uncle. "Stand there, Victor. Hold steady—yes—now wait . . ."

Steve stood up in the boat to watch. The next time the whale came up for air, Victor shot the harpoon into the base of its skull.

"Good!" exclaimed the uncle. "Good shot!"

The dead whale stayed afloat, and the men quickly tied a rope to its tail so they could tow it behind the boat. They began untangling the net.

"*Oogruk!*" exclaimed the cousin. A large bearded seal had snared itself in the net.

In one quick motion, the uncle raised his gun and shot it. Now they had to get the seal into the tossing boat or it would sink.

They sent Liz to sit at the far end of the boat. Then they slowly tilted it until one edge was just inches above the water. Steve leaned over to help, and with a tremendous effort, they hoisted the seal over the side.

Steve sat back, panting. "How big is that thing anyway?"

"Very heavy," said Victor. "May be five hundred pounds."

It took a long time to untangle the net and replace the torn sections with new net, but at last the uncle turned the boat back toward Koyalik. Everyone was smiling.

"Lotsa meat. Lots for everybody," Victor said. He beamed at Liz. "You bring us good luck. Glad to have you."

Liz shook her head and smiled. She pointed to the seal. "What do you call that?"

"*Oogruk,*" said Victor.

Steve looked up from his notebook, then scratched out what he'd written. He smiled to himself. He'd thought *oogruk* meant "Look there."

Slowly they towed the whale back to Koyalik while the sun sank below the water in a bank of glowing clouds. Steve talked to Victor about each piece of equipment in the boat, and as long as he had light to see by, he added new words to his notebook.

It was fully dark by the time they reached Koyalik. Steve took Liz's arm as they climbed the slope to the Trading Post. She moved stiffly, and he knew she must be as cold and tired as he. But Gus had kept a pot of stew for them, along with a plate of his leathery biscuits. Steve ate hungrily and described the whale hunt between mouthfuls.

"Sounds like a beluga," said Gus. "Small, but good eating. They'll carve it up and share it with the whole village." Then he told them that the mail plane had come that afternoon, but there had been nothing for them.

"Wish I'd been here," said Steve. "I've been waiting to meet that pilot."

"Nothing from the Mission," Liz said, sounding disappointed.

"At least our letter went out," said Steve. "They'll get it in a week or two. Then maybe we'll hear something definite."

During the next few days, Steve spent as much time with Victor as he could. They hauled water, chopped wood, and mended Victor's dogsled. And Steve took every chance he could to learn new words.

Victor didn't seem to mind repeating words again and again so Steve could write them down. Sometimes he smiled at the way Steve pronounced a word, but then he'd say, "Keep on, keep on. You learn."

Winter was definitely coming, Steve thought. The river banks had ragged edges of ice, and flocks of geese flew overhead, hurrying south.

Cold drafts blew up between the cracks in the floor of their room. A cup of water left on the washbasin would have a crust of ice by morning. Frost glittered on their windowpanes.

Their room was always cold, even with the little stove burning all day long, and they spent less and less time there. Liz made friends with several of the women besides Nida. She went with them to pick berries and to gather driftwood. One day she helped Nida take the last salmon off the drying rack and stack it, like piles of stiff red logs, in the cache hut beside their cabin.

She had her own Eskimo notebook. Each evening she and Steve sat at the counter in the general store to compare notes. Then they added new words to the thick red binder that was their dictionary.

On Thursday, a stinging west wind brought bad weather that kept the mail plane away, but by evening the clouds had lifted and the wind died down.

Steve was talking to Gus when Liz burst into the Trading Post. "Steve, come look at the mountains! The tops are all white."

To Steve's surprise, Gus put on his parka and followed them outside. "Looks like they got plenty of snow from that last storm," he said. Then he lifted his wrinkled face to the sky. "Can you feel it? Freeze-up tonight."

Darkness fell as they walked down to stand on the edge of the lagoon. For once, the water lay perfectly still, reflecting the stars as tiny points of light.

The old trader sighed in satisfaction. "Forty-two years, I've seen an Alaskan freeze-up. Wouldn't miss it for anything.

He turned to go inside. "Wait till morning. You'll see what I mean."

They stood for a few minutes longer in the dark, biting cold. Liz took Steve's arm. "Look up at the sky," she whispered.

Ruffled curtains of yellow, blue, and green shimmered across the sky. Light fell softly around them; it outlined the tundra grasses and turned the lagoon to silver.

"The Northern Lights," Steve said. "I've never seen them so . . ."

"So beautiful!" said Liz. "The Lord has brought us to a beautiful land."

By morning, the temperature had dropped to eight degrees. The sea, frozen absolutely flat, stretched like a pane of glass to the far horizon. Children were running back and forth on the river ice, shouting.

"Let's go too," said Liz, and picked up her parka.

The river ice was so transparent they could see the mossy stones on the bottom. "There's still some fish down there too," said Liz. "This is amazing."

Now the children held hands and were jumping on the ice. A ringing filled the air. "The ice cry!" they called to each other.

Liz stood still, watching them, and Steve knew she was thinking about the Bible club she wanted to start. She glanced up at him, her blue eyes shining. "See the short one with the red mittens? I talked to him. I told him a story and he liked it. Then I tried it in Eskimo, and he laughed himself silly. He said he might come see us on Sunday."

The little boy wasn't at the church service on Sunday, but Victor's uncle came, and his cousin Henry, and a family who had just returned from their fish camp.

Afterwards, Steve tried to encourage himself. "More families will come back to town now that the river's frozen," he said. "Things will improve." He tried not to think about how long it would be before he could preach in Eskimo.

Nida insisted that they return for supper that evening, and they accepted her offer gratefully.

Victor's cabin, one of the largest in the village, had only two rooms, but Nida kept them spotlessly clean. She welcomed Steve and Liz warmly and served them roast goose with potatoes and carrots from her garden.

When everyone had finished eating, Victor glanced at his wife. She carried over a plate of black, rubbery-looking raw meat, cut into squares. Each piece was topped with a layer of white fat.

"*Muktuk,*" Victor said. He smiled, but his eyes were watchful.

Steve didn't dare look at Liz. He knew how she felt about fatty food. He picked up one of the squares without hesitating, bit into it, and chewed quickly.

It tastes like steak, he thought in surprise. He took another piece and chewed it more slowly. Liz was eating one too.

"This is good," he said to Victor. "What is it?"

"The skin of the whale we caught," said Victor. He looked pleased.

"Amazing," said Liz. She reached for another piece.

They talked late into the evening. Victor and Nida were full of questions about life in Chicago. They seemed to understand when Steve described the tall buildings, and the many streets, and the large lake. But they were curious about the zoo. Nida asked why somebody would keep animals in pens, just to look at. Were there no animals left in the forest?

Finally it was time to go. As Steve and Liz stood up, Nida asked how they liked living at the Trading Post.

"The trader is very good to us," said Steve. "But sometime we would like to find a cabin of our own."

Liz laughed. "When Nida comes to visit, she always ends up dragging me back here to get warm."

Nida pretended to shiver. "Always so cold." Her dark, almond-shaped eyes sparkled. "I think we find you a better house." She looked at her husband. "Okay, Vic?"

On Monday, the plane stayed only long enough to drop off a sack of mail, and Steve didn't get a chance to meet the pilot. But when Gus handed him a packet of mail, he forgot about everything else. One of the letters was a long, grey envelope—from the Mission. He and Liz hurried upstairs to their room, and as soon as the door closed, he slit the envelope open.

"Steve! What's the matter?"

"They said . . . " His voice had gone hoarse. "They said for us to come back."

5 Big Enough

Steve looked back down at the letter and steadied his voice with an effort. "They're very reasonable about it. They know we're not kids just out of school, and that I'm an experienced pilot. But they say we've never lived in Alaska and we've never been missionaries before . . ." He paused, trying to collect his despairing thoughts.

"They're right," he said, and handed the letter to Liz.

She read it silently, her brows drawn into a puzzled frown. Finally she looked up. "No doubt about it—they want us to come back. They're very kind, but . . . " She glanced at the letter. "You know what? It sounds as if they're mostly worried about us. Listen: *It would be irresponsible on our part to expect you to continue alone in such a hazardous field without even a reliable means of transportation.*"

Steve moved to the window. From this height, he could see all the way to the river. On its frozen, gleaming surface, a small figure wearing red mittens skated around and around. A dog scrambled after him.

Steve turned. "Liz, remember the boy I saw out at the airstrip that first morning?"

"Yes." Her eyes glinted with unshed tears.

"If we go back to Chicago and wait until Peter gets well or there's another airplane—or whatever—it might be too late for that boy to hear the gospel."

"And Nida."

"And Victor. He'd be getting old by then."

Steve took a deep breath. "As far as I'm concerned, God still wants us here."

Liz nodded in agreement.

"And the Mission hasn't received our letter yet," he said. "So they don't know that we can't leave right away—because of freeze-up."

He sat down on the trunk, and Liz handed the Mission's letter back to him. "The plan was for us to help Peter, not to pioneer the work—that's true. But if the Lord wants us here, He can supply our needs and show us how to survive."

Liz whispered, *"Have not I commanded thee?"*

He fell silent. Yes, Lord, he thought. You are the One who commanded us and sent us here. But what shall we do about it now? This letter—

"Letters!" he exclaimed. "Grab your pen, Lizzie! We're going to write some letters. Let's see: in Chicago, there's our home church and the other three churches. Then there's your family's church in San Francisco, and all the ones we visited out there. We need some emergency prayer support! There's got to be some way we can convince the Mission to keep this work going."

"Good idea," said Liz. "But let's build up the fire first. And I'm going to put on my parka and gloves. The Mission would not be pleased if I froze to death in my own bedroom."

An hour later, Steve looked up from his work. "Dogs!"

"Dogs?" Liz stopped writing and flexed her gloved fingers.

"Remember I told you about my Uncle Alf? He had a dog team. Used to take me along when he checked his trap lines. Lots of times he let me drive the team."

Steve folded the letter he had just written and stood up to put more wood on the fire. "Everyone around here has dog teams. We can get to other villages by dogsled. We don't *have* to have an airplane."

He grinned at Liz. "You know why flying is more dangerous than traveling by dogsled?"

"I don't trust that look on your face, Steve Bailey. Okay, I'll bite. Why?"

"Because in an emergency you can't eat your airplane."

"Oh, Steve! I couldn't *ever* eat my dog!" Liz bent over to pull on an extra pair of socks. "Where'd you hear a horrible thing like that?"

"Gus told me—the Eskimos say that. What are you doing?"

"Freezing! My feet are blocks of ice. I'm going to climb into my sleeping bag if we stay in here much longer."

"We can finish up later," said Steve. "The mail won't go out until Thursday. But I'm going to write the Mission about traveling by dogsled. Let's talk to the Lord before we go downstairs."

They huddled on the trunk, and Steve prayed about the Mission's letter and his idea of using a dog team. At the end he said, "Thank you for bringing us to these people, Lord. Show us what to do—today."

Liz reached for his hand as they walked down the splintered old staircase. "I think the Lord's going to get us a dog team, Steve."

He nodded, hoping she was right. Dogs were expensive, and so were sleds. It wouldn't be easy.

"Maybe we could ask Victor about some dogs," he said.

They found Victor outside his cabin, repairing his cache hut. His dogs, each chained to a post, watched him alertly. Two of them jumped up and down, yelping with eagerness. Liz nudged Steve.

Those huskies are ready to run, he thought. He eyed their smooth fur and muscular legs. Well cared-for, too.

Victor looked up with a smile. "I wonder what happen to you. Nida say maybe you frozen stiff in that room."

"We're fine," said Steve, still thinking about the dogs.

Victor hammered in one more nail. "May be, we find you house."

Steve wasn't sure what he meant. "Do people around here ever rent out cabins?"

Victor looked puzzled. "Rent? Oh." He shook his head. "Not rent. Sometimes sell. Best way—to get one nobody use."

"I saw one that looks empty—over by the airstrip," said Liz. "Oh, there's Nida. Hi!"

"Hi to you." Nida gave them her bright smile. "That cabin with lock? White woman. She go away. Think we steal her stuff. May be. So she put big lock on door." Nida glanced at Victor. "You tell them?"

"I will tell," said Victor firmly, and Nida went back into the cabin. Victor gazed at Steve and Liz for a long moment, then he said, "There is house, if you want."

Liz exclaimed in delight, and he raised a hand. "Not very big. Not very nice. Might not be okay for white mans."

"We'd be glad to look at it," said Steve. "Who owns it?"

"Nobody." Victor looked uncomfortable. He put down his hammer. "Used to be old man lived there. Now . . . nobody."

"Okay," said Steve. Why did Victor sound so hesitant?

"I show you." They followed Victor a short distance through the village to a small cabin on the edge of the tundra. It was built of peeled spruce logs like most of the others and weathered to silver by the wind. There was no storm porch on the front. Perhaps that was why no one wanted it, Steve thought.

The windows and sloping roof looked quite ordinary, and it was set low in the ground, Eskimo fashion. Blocks of grassy earth covered the lower part of the walls.

Steve touched Liz's arm. "See how the sod keeps out the wind, down near the floor? No cold feet in that house."

Victor had to lean against the door to get it open. He peered inside. "Might be little bit cold until you get fixed."

Steve and Liz walked inside, and immediately Steve saw what he meant. The chinking had fallen out between the logs along one wall. Someone had tried to patch the larger holes with wads of newspaper, but the paper crumbled when Steve poked a finger into it.

Victor still stood in the doorway. "That stuff no good. Get moss."

The other walls were covered with soot-smeared cardboard, crudely cut out around the two small windows. Colorful but tattered pages from magazines were tacked to the cardboard.

A wide shelf jutted out from the back wall. Or maybe that was a bed, Steve thought. It could use some struts for support.

Liz smiled up at him. "This looks big enough for us, don't you think, Steve?"

"Right. We don't need anything fancy." He walked toward a jumble of furniture in one corner. A homemade chair. And a square table lying on its side. Good. He set the table upright, and it teetered on three legs.

Liz lifted a pile of dusty hides off the large black stove that squatted against the back wall. "Look at this."

He laughed. "Ought to keep us plenty warm."

Liz put down the hides and joined him in the middle of the room. "What is that smell?" she asked in a low voice.

"Seal oil," said Victor from the doorway. "Someone spilled in here. Scrub floor, it go away. That old man—" He stopped abruptly. "Out back, come see shed."

The dark little shed that leaned against the cabin's back wall was piled with odds and ends. Nothing much there, Steve thought, but they could clean out the place and use it for storage.

He exchanged a glance with Liz. "The cabin will be just fine," he said. "Thank you very much, Victor."

Victor seemed to be in a hurry to get back to his work. "Okay, good, I help you get moss for walls."

That evening, back in their room at the Trading Post, Steve and Liz discussed the cabin. "You don't mind that it's small and sort of primitive?" he asked. "I don't want to be the kind of missionary who lives in a fancy house."

"It's okay," said Liz. "And we can fix it up. I'd like to tear down the cardboard and wipe off those logs. The new moss chinking will help a lot."

"Yes; we've got to find out where they get it. Probably out on the tundra somewhere."

"And the floor," Liz said. "That seal oil smells awful fishy."

Steve nodded. "The floor, first thing. I can fix that table and build us another couple of chairs. I saw shelves, but we'll need some more."

"You know what," said Liz slowly, "I wonder why Victor had that odd look on his face when he talked about the old man. And he never really came inside the cabin."

"Strange, isn't it?" said Steve. "Hey, I forgot to ask him about dogs."

"Maybe tomorrow." Liz finished washing her face and crawled into her sleeping bag. "What did you say you two are going to do tomorrow?"

"Victor's taking his dog team out for a run. He's going to deliver some seal oil to his brother, the one who lives up the river. He asked if I wanted to come along."

"His dog team, huh? I wonder what you'll find to talk about . . ."

Steve grinned. "You guessed it."

6 The Huskies

The next morning, Steve arrived early at Victor's cabin. Victor was harnessing his excited, yipping dogs, moving from one to the next with practiced ease.

Steve stood silent, remembering. It had been years since he'd driven a dog team, but he was aching to try.

Victor tucked one of his small boys under caribou furs on the sled and gave him the seal oil to hold, then they were ready.

"*Gih!*" shouted Victor, and the huskies shot off across the ice. Steve swung into a rhythmic trot that carried him along behind them.

The river crossed the tundra like a broad avenue of ice, then curved toward the mountains. The ice was smooth, and the huskies galloped easily along it, swinging their plumed tails high.

After an hour, Victor guided the team onto a flat, snow-covered ledge beside the river. He was stopping to give the dogs a rest, and it was none too soon for Steve. Each dog dropped instantly to the snow. Steve felt like doing the same.

"Dogs not used to working," said Victor.

"Neither am I," Steve said. "It's been a long time since I've run behind a dogsled."

Silently, Victor built a fire and boiled coffee in a smoke-blackened coffee can that was equipped with wire handles. After a while, he asked, "You have dogs, in Chicago?"

"My uncle had a team. In Minnesota," Steve said. "You know, I've been thinking I'd like to get some dogs and put together a team of my own."

Victor nodded. He adjusted the crotched stick that held the coffee pot. He straightened one of the dogs' harnesses, then he gazed into the thicket of snow-frosted willows beside the river.

Steve bit his lip, waiting. What was it Gus had told him? "Never try to hurry an Eskimo."

Finally Victor said, "Saw you looking at my dogs." He handed Steve a cup of steaming coffee. "Think I better lock them up tonight." He grinned.

"You've got a good team," said Steve. "I can tell that you take care of them."

They drank their coffee in silence, and soon Victor got the dogs back onto their feet. He motioned Steve to stand behind the sled on one of the runners, and Steve was glad to accept the invitation. Victor stood on a runner too, but the huskies didn't seem to mind the extra weight. They pulled at top speed, and the rest of the trip went quickly.

Victor's brother lived in a small village close to the river. He had a large number of dogs chained behind his cabin, and Victor took Steve back to look at them.

"My brother raise dogs to sell," Victor said, and mentioned some prices. "See here." They walked to a group of six young huskies chained next to each other.

Victor's brother didn't speak English, so Victor explained. "He train these for a man who live in Nome. All belong to same litter, so don't fight as much."

The dogs were beautifully marked and seemed to be in top condition. Someone in Nome with plenty of money was going to have a first-rate team, Steve thought.

He studied the rest of the huskies while Victor talked to his brother. Excellent dogs, he thought, but too expensive for me. Victor didn't say anything about buying dogs from his brother, and Steve was careful not to mention it.

On the trip back, Victor talked about adventures he'd had with his favorite dogs, and Steve shared some tales of his own. It wasn't until they had almost reached Koyalik that Victor said anything more about a dog team for Steve.

"May be I find you some dogs. You rich?"

Steve grinned.

Victor grinned too. "Good dogs cost lotsa money. Or trade for furs."

He paused, and Steve waited. The young Eskimo knew he had no extra money and no furs.

"Well, I look around. I think you need five dogs."

"I can build a sled—" Steve began.

Victor smiled. "We make sled together."

The next morning, Victor took a look at the sky and announced that they'd better get the moss for the cabin. "More snow come. Too deep for find moss." He showed Steve where to find it, out on the tundra, and they filled several bags with the brown, fuzzy plants. They piled them onto Victor's sled and bumped over the scanty snow, back to the village.

Meanwhile, Liz had torn down the cardboard and started cleaning the logs. They worked late that night by the light of a kerosene lantern. As they trudged slowly back to the Trading Post, snowflakes glistened in the beam of Steve's flashlight.

Liz slipped her arm into his. "Victor was right about the snow. But we're almost finished fixing up our cabin, and then we won't care how much it snows."

It snowed that night and all the next day, enough to keep the mail plane from landing. But as soon as they could stamp out a path to their cabin, Steve and Liz went back to work on it. Between cleaning sessions, they visited one of the English-speaking families and prayed about the dog team. And during the long, dark evenings, Victor and Steve spent hours at Victor's cabin, working on a sled.

Late Saturday evening, they moved a few things into the cabin so they could stay overnight. Steve stood in the middle of the room and gazed around himself with satisfaction. The kerosene lantern cast a golden light over the freshly cleaned logs. Pots glinted from the kitchen corner, where Liz had hung them. The stove crackled with plenty of warmth.

"It'll take time," he said, thinking about the crates still stacked at the Trading Post. "But the Lord has given us a good start."

Liz, already in bed, mumbled in drowsy agreement.

On Sunday morning, there were no new faces at the service, but each person listened intently. Steve spoke in English, then Victor translated. Steve found it hard to compose his ideas and listen to what Victor was saying at the same time.

It's going to take me forever to learn this language, he thought. I know a couple of words, but I still haven't figured out how they go together.

Monday morning, the mail plane made its usual low pass over the airstrip. Then it turned and landed, its skis bumping over the icy snow.

Steve made sure he was down there by the time the plane taxied to a stop. A cluster of children waited too, looking expectant, and as soon as the pilot climbed out, they surrounded him.

Young and blond and good-looking, he clearly was a big favorite. The children crowded close, all chattering at once, and some even hung onto his brown leather jacket. He bent low to talk to them for a few minutes, then he handed out the freight.

One by one, the children carried packages up to the Trading Post, and Steve moved closer. "Need a hand?"

"Sure." Friendly blue eyes glanced up at him. "This mail-bag is too heavy for those kids."

By the time Steve got back down from the Trading Post, the pilot was knotting the plane's tie-down ropes. The sunlight gleamed on a scar that curved down one side of his face. He turned at the sound of Steve's crunching steps in the snow.

"Hi, my name's Jackson." He held out a hand, and Steve took it.

"Steve Bailey."

Jackson smiled. "The missionary, right? Friend of Pete's. Are you a pilot too?"

"Yes," said Steve. "Haven't done any flying up here, though."

Jackson shook his head. "Bad, bad news about Pete," he said. "Could have happened to any of us."

He lifted out one last box and patted the airplane's red fuselage. "Ever fly one of these babies?"

Steve grinned. "Flew one in regular service—the job I had before I came up here—but not on skis."

They walked up to the Trading Post together. Jackson must have injured his leg, Steve thought. He slowed his pace to match the young pilot's limping gait.

Gus persuaded them both to stay for a cup of coffee, and they talked for a short time until Jackson had to hurry off.

That evening, they were unpacking their trunk when Victor knocked at the door. Behind him were three dogs on a rope. "Not the best," he said. "Everyone want to keep good dogs."

All three huskies were thin and scruffy looking, but Steve knew that the Eskimo didn't bother much with their dogs during the summer. He and Liz thanked Victor and asked him to come in for a cup of tea. The young Eskimo seemed reluctant, so they didn't insist. After he left, they tied up the dogs behind the cabin and spent some time with them.

"Remember, they're not pets," Steve said to Liz. "They're work animals, so don't get too attached."

He examined the dogs carefully. One of them, at least, seemed young and alert. But both his ears were torn and his face was scarred. A fighter. Probably a troublemaker.

Liz named him Bandit because of the black mask on his face.

The second dog had a muscular body, but one eye was missing. Steve didn't notice at first because fur had grown over the empty socket. The dog seemed to get along fine with one eye.

"That spot of black fur looks like a patch over his eye," said Liz. "I'm going to call him Patch."

The third husky curled up and went to sleep immediately. Steve thought he looked sick, but he didn't say anything to Liz. She had named him Droopy.

The next evening, Victor brought them two more dogs, both with shaggy brown coats. "Strays," he said. "Hanging around, stealing food. Pretty soon, somebody shoot them."

The pair looked half-dead. They moved stiffly over the frozen ground with their tails between their legs. One was so thin that his legs looked like sticks of wood. An open wound marred one ear, but he had long, powerful legs and large paws. Liz named him Bigfoot.

The other dog had a mournful look about him, and he spent all night singing to the moon. By midnight, Liz was calling him The Dreadful Howler.

The next morning, Steve and Liz lingered over their breakfast and spent some extra time in prayer. They thanked the Lord for the dogs and asked for wisdom in training them.

Steve began working with the dogs right away. At first he tried Bandit as leader, then he tried Bigfoot. The big brown stray was more obedient and willing than Bandit, so he kept him in the lead. To his relief, the rest of the dogs pulled well together and usually obeyed his commands.

The next day, he and Victor took their teams out to haul ice and to cut wood. With each trip, it seemed to Steve that his team improved.

Victor said he was going back up the river to see his brother on Thursday, and Steve decided to take the team on its first long trip. Liz wanted to come too, so he'd let her ride in the sled.

Early Thursday morning, Liz went out to feed the dogs as usual, but she came back in a hurry. "Steve, come look at Droopy. There's something terribly wrong with him."

7 Mikki

Steve reached for his parka. "What's the matter with him?"

"Well, I threw that dried salmon out for them like always, and . . . and . . . he didn't jump up. He didn't even move." Liz shivered in spite of her heavy jacket. "I couldn't bear to go any closer."

He found the dog still curled up in the snow. It must have died in its sleep. "Droopy was sick," he said. He put an arm around Liz. "Don't worry," he said gently. "Perhaps the Lord will send us another dog."

But the lifeless form in the snow reminded him that they lived in a harsh country.

Lord, You know we needed that dog, he prayed silently. Well, maybe not that dog—maybe an even better one. A leader. Help me to trust You for a good team.

On the trip upriver, Steve had trouble making his dogs keep up with Victor's team.

It couldn't be from Liz riding on the sled, he thought. They're just not pulling together very well.

When he stopped the team for a rest, Bandit snarled and lunged toward Bigfoot. Steve shouted at them and snatched up his whip in case the other dogs joined in. He grabbed Bandit just as he sank his teeth into the big brown husky's neck.

"I'm going to move this rascal," Steve said to Liz. He harnessed Bandit into the wheel position, in front of the sled. "Maybe some hard work will keep him from picking fights."

Victor had been watching. "You need good leader," he said. "This brown one okay, but he afraid of the one who fight him. Good leader is boss and make team work harder."

"I think you're right," said Steve. "I'm praying for a really good dog."

Victor's eyebrows went up. "May be find another stray by side of river?"

Steve smiled and said nothing. But as they started off, he prayed again about the team.

Victor's brother seemed to have more dogs than ever, although the matched team of six was gone. He pointed out several others that he was training.

"I love huskies," exclaimed Liz. "They're such beautiful dogs. How much do these cost, Steve?"

"Too much, Lizzie. Way too much for us."

"Look at that grey one with the floppy ear! He's young, isn't he? He's got such intelligent eyes!"

"Hmm. Looks like a wolf, with those markings. Kind of small," said Steve.

"Maybe Victor could find out whether he's for sale."

"Liz—"

But Victor was already talking to his brother.

Liz stood on tiptoe to whisper in Steve's ear. "My birthday money from Mom, remember? Twenty-five dollars. I brought it along, just in case."

"My brother say okay to sell. Not very much," said Victor.

"What's the matter with the dog?" Steve hoped Liz wouldn't interrupt.

"Something wrong with ear."

Great, Steve thought. I've got a half-blind dog already. A deaf one will fit right in.

Liz was squeezing his hand.

"What does he mean?" Steve asked carefully. "Is the dog deaf?"

Victor smiled. "No, not deaf." To demonstrate, he clapped his hands beside the dog's head. The grey husky stepped aside quickly and glanced at Victor.

"Just crooked ear," Victor said. "See how it flop down?"

Victor's brother said something, and Victor translated. "White man want perfect dog. He send this one back."

"He's pretty small," said Steve. "How old?"

"More than one year. My brother already train him. You have American dollar? My brother like that best of all."

"Ask him how much. I can give him American dollars right here and now. But not very many."

As Victor translated, his brother's eyes gleamed. He made a long speech and smiled at Steve.

"American dollar—he want twenty. My brother say he give you special price."

Steve looked at Liz. "I'm not going to haggle."

She smiled. "Okay."

"What do you think, Vic?" asked Steve.

"He have good big feet. Can run with bad ear. Feed him right, he grow little bit."

They harnessed the new dog with Steve's team for the trip back, and both men watched to see how he behaved. By the time they reached Koyalik, Victor was nodding approval.

"Good," he said. "May be very good when he grow up."

Steve agreed. "Looks like one smart cookie to me. What're you going to name him, Liz?

"He needs an Eskimo name." She turned to Victor. "How do you say 'He does a good job even though he's small' "?

Victor thought for a moment. "We say *mik-shrok*," he said at last. "That mean 'small-but-good enough.' "

"Perfect!" exclaimed Liz. "We'll call him Mikki for short."

That evening, they stopped by the Trading Post to tell Gus about the new husky. "If the dog came from Victor's brother, it's going to be a good one," said Gus. "You got some mail this morning."

"That's right; it's Thursday," said Steve. "I lose track of the days. Wish I hadn't missed Jackson."

"He was in a hurry this time," Gus said. "A real worker, that boy. Did you know he's got a box full of medals from the war? Our very own World War II flying ace. That's how he banged up his leg." The old trader shuffled through the mail, still talking. "One of these days he'll stay long enough for a real visit. Especially if you mention food. Here's your letter."

The letter was from Peter, and they waited until they got back to the cabin to open it. After Steve had built up the fire and put on a kettle of water to boil, he read it to Liz.

Peter was still in the hospital. He needed another operation, and then he'd start physical therapy. But he said he felt stronger every day. He'd written to tell them about the Eskimo village he'd discovered the week before his accident.

> It's fairly big, on the north shore of Mierow Lake. I flew over it one day and stopped to visit out of curiosity. These people seem to know about Christ, but they're hungry for good teaching—very open and friendly. Many of them speak English. If there's any way you could get there, you'd have a great ministry! I don't know how far it is from Koyalik, but Gus or Victor could tell you.

Then Peter asked about Victor and the few families that had been coming to church. At the end of the letter, he added,

> P.S. Found a great price on some Bibles. I'm sending you a few—Praying that you can use them—maybe at Mierow Lake. P.P.S.—I'm sure an airplane would be a big help to the ministry. I'm praying about that too.

Steve looked up from the letter. "This sounds exciting!"

Liz poured tea and sat down beside him. "What are you thinking?"

"Well, it seems to me that we can't do much here in Koyalik until we learn the language better. That could take months. But what's-it-called—" He glanced back at the letter. "Mierow Lake sounds like a wonderful opportunity."

"Victor might know something about it," said Liz. "We could ask him and Nida over supper and have a good talk. I've been wanting to invite them—they've never even visited us here. Why don't you ask him tomorrow, when you go to hunt ptarmigan?"

The next day after they had shot a half-dozen of the plump white birds, Steve told Victor about Liz's invitation.

For a minute the young Eskimo didn't answer. He sighted down his rifle, then he polished the barrel with his sleeve. "It better you come to our house," he said at last. "We take Nida lotsa birds; she want to have feast."

When Steve told Liz, she frowned.

"Well, that's odd," she said. "You know what? The other women don't come visit me here like they did at the Trading Post. And the children—they'll peek in the windows, but they won't come inside. I'm going to ask Nida what's the matter. She's not the strong, silent type like Victor. She'll tell me."

That evening, however, it was Victor who explained. Liz must have said something about the cabin to Nida while they were fixing supper, Steve thought.

As they were finishing the meal, Nida gave Victor one of her bright smiles. She said quietly, "We tell about the old man's cabin."

Victor picked up his cup, then put it down again. "May be nothing wrong with cabin. But I tell you. An old man die in there."

He stopped and looked pleadingly at Steve and Liz. "This not bother white mans. But Eskimo, he think about the *tungat*. After old man die, no one take care of his spirit properly."

Victor gazed at a spot above Steve's head. "Taboo . . ."

It must have been too difficult to explain in English, for he shrugged and hurried on. "Now may be old man spirit still in cabin. Angry. *Tungat* make Eskimo sick or even dead."

"So that's why no one in the village will come to visit," said Liz slowly.

"They watch," said Nida. "If you don't get sick, after a while, they know *tungat* go away. Not angry. Then people come." She glanced sideways at Victor. "For a little bit, keep church at our house. They come here okay."

"Thank you," said Steve. "We didn't understand."

Nida asked what people in the States liked to eat at the end of a meal, and for a while they talked about desserts. Liz described some of her favorites, and both Victor and Nida listened with interest.

They were always eager to learn about the white man's ways, Steve thought. More than anyone else in the village.

After a while, he asked Victor about Mierow Lake.

"Yes, go upriver, then into mountains. Maybe two—three sleeps."

"That's not too bad," said Steve.

"You want go sometime?" asked Victor. "Tomorrow I go to my trap line—two weeks. May be when I get back."

That night, Steve lay awake for a long time, thinking and praying about the Eskimos at Mierow Lake. Two sleeps meant a three-day trip if all went well. Back in Minnesota, he'd taken the dogs out for a week at a time. But this was Alaska. These dogs weren't experienced, and they weren't very fast. He'd better talk to Gus.

For the next few days, Steve worked the dogs hard and fed them well. Each morning they got dried salmon, and each evening Liz filled their pans with her special mixture of boiled rice and meat leftovers. She kept the best tidbits for Mikki. "He smacks his lips when he sees me coming," she said. "Like a hungry kid!"

Steve took the team out onto the ice to train them. Mikki ran with all his heart and managed to keep up with the older dogs. Bandit kept picking fights, especially with Bigfoot. The big stray wasn't the best leader in the world, but he'd have to do. Were they ready for a long trip? Maybe.

Monday afternoon, Steve stopped in to ask Gus about Mierow Lake. The old man's eyes brightened. "Used to hunt caribou up there a lot—it's right on the migration path. Why do you want to go so badly?" He threw Steve a sharp glance. "That's right—you've got that preaching you like to do. Well, if you wait for Victor, it'll be a month or more. Eskimos don't think of time the way we do."

Gus scratched at his beard, thinking. He looked down at the group of men gathered around the stove. Then he called out something in a language that sounded different from Eskimo.

A tall, shaggy-haired man strolled over to the counter. Gus took a long time asking him a question.

Finally, Gus turned to Steve. "This man is going past Mierow Lake, he says. He's an Indian; knows the country well. He can show you the way."

The Indian said something hurriedly.

"If you want to go, he's leaving first thing in the morning."

Steve hesitated. "Does he speak English?"

The Indian smiled. "Yes, yes. English. Good dogs too."

"My dogs aren't very fast," said Steve.

The man smiled widely, showing brown-stained teeth. "Okay. Leave early, before sun. Two dollar."

Steve looked at the old trader.

"That's a good price," said Gus.

After he'd settled the details with the Indian, Steve hurried to tell Liz. She agreed that it seemed like a good opportunity. "But you're sure you can't wait for Victor?"

"Wait!" exclaimed Steve. "That's all we ever do! If it isn't the weather, it's something else." He pulled back his impatience and tried to explain. "I've got to grab every chance

I get or we'll never accomplish anything—and the Mission will send us back for sure."

He packed the sled carefully with provisions for the trip, plus extras in case of bad weather. They made plans for Liz to stay at Nida's house, since Victor was away too.

That night Steve fed the dogs an especially hearty supper, then he lay awake half the night, worrying that he'd forget to get up in time.

But he remembered, and early the next morning he met the Indian at the Trading Post. Steve paid him one of the two dollars, and they started off.

The Indian's dogs were large and well-trained, and they soon left Steve's team behind. He didn't let it bother him. Although the sun hadn't risen, the moon gave plenty of light. The ice was in good shape, and his dogs rushed eagerly over its gleaming, silver expanse. It felt wonderful to be mushing again.

Just past the village where Victor's brother lived, he caught up with the Indian. The man had started a fire and boiled coffee while he rested his dogs. He smiled at Steve and silently handed him a cup of coffee. Long before Steve was ready to leave, the Indian jumped to his feet, said something to his dogs, and disappeared down the river.

The next time Steve saw him, it was midafternoon. The sun had risen late, and now it hung low over the mountains, wreathed in clouds.

The Indian was not smiling. "Hurry more," he said, glancing at the sky.

"My dogs are tired," said Steve. "Why don't we stop for the night?"

"No stop now. We go to tall rocks, then stop." The man drank the rest of his coffee in one gulp. "I wait for you there. If I miss you, just follow river. At tall rocks, go north."

He was out of sight before Steve had untangled his dogs' harnesses. "We'll be okay," he said to the team. He swung them back onto the ice. "*Gih,* Bigfoot! Watch for tall rocks, you guys."

The dogs leaped ahead with new energy. Steve stood on the sled's runners, and the snow-frosted tundra slid quietly past. The mountains came closer and closer.

That's probably where the tall rocks are, thought Steve. I'll be glad to get there.

The dogs began to slow, and he stepped off the sled so they wouldn't have to pull his weight.

The next time he glanced up at the mountains, they were veiled in fog. Minutes later, fog swirled down the river toward them, quiet and cool and grey. Soon the dogs ran in a whirling mist. All Steve could see of them was their tails moving faintly through the grey.

We've got to keep on, he thought. We've got to stay on the river. He shouted to Bigfoot, and the dogs ran faster.

Suddenly the sled swerved. Bigfoot was taking it up the riverbank.

The team rushed across the grey-white expanse of the tundra, and Steve could not stop them. He stood on the brake, but the snow wasn't deep enough for it to grab. He yelled until he was hoarse, but still they raced on.

The wind blew up, down, sideways, from all directions at once. It picked up snow from the ground and flung the needle-sharp, icy particles into his face.

The temperature dropped steadily as the wind gained speed, and Steve's hands began to go numb in spite of his fur mittens. The sled bumped crazily over tussocks of frozen tundra grass. It was all he could do to hold on.

8 Kuyana

The dogs began to slow.

They must be deathly tired, Steve thought. But he couldn't make camp out here. They had to keep going. He peered into the whirling grey dusk that surrounded them. Nothing.

The dogs stopped. "No!" he yelled. "You can't give up on me," Steve yelled. They ignored him and began to dig down between the snowy tussocks, out of the wind. "Bigfoot, where are you?"

He couldn't see through the snow, so he felt his way along the towline. If he could just get the leader up and moving—

He stumbled over Bigfoot's hunched back and fell against the door of a cabin.

A moment later, the door opened and someone motioned him inside. The door closed behind him, and he stood breathless in the sudden quiet. The room was dim and warm. He stripped off his mittens and beat his hands together, trying to coax some feeling back into them.

An old Eskimo man took him by the arm and led him close to the stove. "Thank you," Steve said. "I don't know how we got here, but my dogs suddenly took off—we were lost in the fog on the river, trying to get to the tall rocks the Indian told me about, and one minute the sky was clear, then the wind started to blow . . ." He stopped, conscious that he was babbling.

The room seemed to be full of people. Dark eyes watched him from weathered brown faces, but obviously, no one had understood a word he said.

He flexed his hands in the warmth of the room and tried to think of the Eskimo words he had learned. Table? chair? cabin?—no, those wouldn't do. Oh, yes—"*Kuyana* (thank you)."

Smiles appeared, all around. One little girl giggled. He probably hadn't said it right.

His fingers tingled painfully. He wanted to take off his heavy parka, to sleep . . . How in the world had Bigfoot known . . . The dogs! They must be starving hungry!

He couldn't remember the Eskimo word for dogs, so he said "Dogs!" and pointed outside. He pulled on his mittens and turned back into the snow-filled darkness. One of the men came along to help.

The dogs didn't want to move, but they stirred when he shouted to them, and finally he got them fed and securely chained. He grabbed his sleeping bag and a bag of food from the sled and tried to repack everything else tightly. By the time he finished, the dogs were curled up again. Each one had its rump to the wind and its nose tucked under its bushy tail.

Once he was back inside, the family studied him in kindly silence. There were no chairs, so he sat stiffly on the floor. One of the women picked up a white mug and poured something out of it into a bucket. She spit on the mug's brown stains, rubbed hard with a rag, then filled it with hot black tea. She handed the mug to him with a smile, and Steve took it gratefully.

Soon he felt warm enough to take off his parka. Then he opened his bag of food. The children—at least five of them—gathered round, watching his every move. He handed the woman a package of Liz's peanut butter cookies. She smiled and said something that sounded a little like *"Kuyana."* Then she gave a cookie to each child. The oldest one sniffed at her cookie first, like a puppy, and said something in Eskimo. Soon they were all smiling as they crunched on their cookies.

The woman said something to him that he could not understand and brought him a bowl of dark, meaty stew. He spooned up some oddly shaped pieces that made him wonder what was in it, but he didn't let that stop him. It tasted fine—hot and savory and filling.

He ate slowly, listening to the wind howl around the cabin. The air inside was stuffy, almost too warm, and thick with the smell of fish and sweating bodies. But anything was better than being outside. The Lord had brought him safely here . . . where was he, anyway?

The woman sent the children into the other room, probably to bed. Then she sat down again, but she glanced at the door from time to time.

He unrolled his sleeping bag in a corner and crawled into it, hoping that he was out of the way. The adults talked by the stove, and the soft purring syllables of Eskimo washed through his tired mind. He fell asleep in the middle of praying for Liz.

Hours later, perhaps early morning, he awoke. All around him, Eskimos lay sleeping, wrapped in caribou hides. He struggled into his parka and mittens and went out to check on the dogs.

The wind still blew, sending flurries of snow across the frozen ground with a thin, rustling sound. The dogs slept unmoving, and he did not try to rouse them. He went back inside and fell asleep instantly.

He awoke when a man came into the cabin, kicking snow off his boots. This was a different face. The woman rose to meet him and said something in Eskimo.

The man cocked his head at Steve. "Eeenglish?"

"Yes, well, actually, I'm American. But do you speak English?"

"Little bit, may be."

Steve soon found that it was a very little bit, but the man seemed to understand fairly well. His name was Joseph, and he was the father of this family.

Steve described how the storm had caught them and Bigfoot had taken off on his own.

Joseph didn't look surprised. "The dogs, they know. In storm, I let my dogs go."

They talked some more together, then Steve ate with the family. He learned that he was in the village of Shanaluk. The tall rocks were cliffs near the river, not far away. But when he asked about Mierow Lake, Joseph didn't seem to know where it might be.

Steve sighed inwardly. I'll have to go back to Koyalik, he thought. What a waste of time!

In the afternoon, the wind died down, and visitors stopped at the cabin. A few teenagers came too. They sat at the back of the room and watched Steve, whispering to each other.

Word must be getting around, Steve thought. Makes me feel like I'm on display in the zoo. But what a chance to preach the gospel! I wonder if Joseph could translate for me.

When he asked, Joseph nodded. "Okay."

Steve began by telling a little about himself. He tried to keep his words simple and the sentences short. He told about the storm and how God had brought him to Shanaluk.

The Eskimos watched him carefully and seemed to be listening, but their faces were blank.

That's odd, thought Steve.

Soon Joseph seemed to tire of the effort, and his translations grew shorter and shorter. The visitors began to leave. One of the last to go was a slender teenager with lively, curious eyes. He stopped beside Steve on his way out. "You come back and talk more?"

"I hope so," said Steve.

The boy left, and after the door closed behind him, Steve realized that the young Eskimo had spoken in English.

By the next morning, the weather had cleared enough for him to travel, and he said *"Kuyana"* to the woman once more. He'd been practicing, and no one giggled this time.

As the miles slid by, Steve had time to think. He shouldn't have rushed off to look for Mierow Lake. He knew that now. So he'd wasted all this time and energy. Or had he? Maybe the Lord could use it for good.

Have not I commanded thee? The verse crept into his mind, both a rebuke and an encouragement.

Yes, Lord, *You're* the one in charge here, he prayed. Forgive me for being so impatient.

The dogs ran well, and he reached Koyalik before sunset. Liz was happily surprised to see him return so soon.

She hurried to warm up some stew while he told her what had happened. After he finished the story, he brought in another armload of wood for the stove. "I was an idiot to go off on my own like that. The Lord was very merciful, the way He led me to Shanaluk."

"Thanks to our Bigfoot," said Liz. "I've heard of dogs knowing where to go in a storm. I wonder if he used to live around that village."

"We'll probably never know," said Steve.

"Did Bandit start any fights?"

"No, he was probably too cold."

"How did Mikki do?"

Steve smiled. "He worked hard to keep up with the big boys, and he did fine. You would have been proud. The other day, Victor said I should move him up next to the leader. Maybe next time I'll try it."

Liz looked up from the pot she was stirring. "Next time? When's that?"

"Soon as I can get away. Remember the boy I told you about, the one who talked to me? His face was so eager and afraid and curious, all at the same time. I've got to go back."

"Wish I could come."

"Well, you could, except you'd have to sleep on the floor with all those people. That's not so good."

"I guess not," said Liz. "Here, this is ready."

"I like your stew," Steve said with a laugh. "Maybe because I know what's in it."

While they ate, Steve thought about Shanaluk. Then he said, "How about this: when Victor gets back, we'll try to find the place they call Tall Rocks. We can set up camp there and then go visit Shanaluk together."

"Good idea," said Liz. After a minute she smiled at him. "Don't tell me you're going to sit here peacefully for who-knows-how-many weeks until Victor gets back."

"Well, I'm sure there's plenty to do," Steve said. "I can visit some families and work on our dictionary. I've got a couple of the dogs' harnesses to mend. I can build your shelves and maybe even a few chairs too. But without Victor . . ."

He took another bite of stew and chewed it slowly. "This is really good."

"It's Nida's recipe; she adds wild celery. You know what? Yesterday afternoon, some children came to her cabin. They loved my big picture book with the bears in it."

Steve's thoughts wandered back to Shanaluk. "The children liked your cookies. I wonder if I would've had pictures—or one of your picture books . . . they might have understood better. I wish you could have seen that boy's face . . ." He stopped.

Liz was smiling at him. "Okay, so when are you going back?"

He had to smile too. "Well, I don't want to be gone over Sunday. How about Monday morning? Do you mind? Could you stay with Nida, just for that one night?"

"I'll start baking cookies!"

Sunday night, a storm swept in from the Bering Sea. The wind and the tide beat at the shore ice, breaking it up and driving it into ridges and mountains of ice. Monday was worse. All day they listened to the shriek and clamor of shattering, grinding ice. The temperature fell to forty degrees below zero, and no one in the village ventured out into the cutting wind.

By Thursday, the sky had cleared, and Steve began to plan once more for his trip to Shanaluk. He and Liz had prayed much during the storm, and he felt confident that he could accomplish something this time. He packed the sled carefully, and in his duffle bag he put one of Liz's books that showed large, colorful pictures of animals.

He left Friday morning before sunrise. This time he tried Howler as the lead dog and put Mikki just behind him. The team seemed to run faster than ever. The ice was slick, swept clear of snow and polished smooth by the wind. They reached Shanaluk by late afternoon.

Joseph's cabin was on the outskirts of the village, and Steve found it without difficulty. The village was bigger than he'd thought. Behind it was a small lake and the mountains he'd seen from the river.

He had planned to drive on past Joseph's, but the cabin door opened and five children rushed out. While Steve was trying to remember the Eskimo word for "Hello," Joseph stepped outside too. "You come back?" He smiled broadly. "You stay?"

"Just for a visit," said Steve.

"Come in, come in."

By the time Steve had unharnessed the dogs and fed them, a small group of Eskimos had gathered inside the cabin. He showed them the book he had brought and talked about its bright pictures. After each sentence, he had to wait for Joseph to translate.

The boy was there again, at the back of the room. He seemed to be listening, his dark eyes intent. Once he smiled to himself. But the rest of the people looked confused.

Steve turned the pages slowly, choosing simple words and trying to emphasize that God created these animals. After the last picture he waited, hoping someone would ask a question. No one did. A few women spoke quietly to Joseph's wife, but the men started going outside.

The boy got up to leave, and Steve headed for the door too, hoping to catch up with him. But children were playing underfoot, and two large women stood in his way. When he finally reached the door and stepped out into the cold, dark night, the boy had disappeared.

9 Storm Coming

That evening, several men came to Joseph's cabin, but Steve soon realized that they hadn't come because of him. Each one gave Steve a polite smile, then joined the others around the stove.

Joseph poured something into cups and passed them around. He brought a cup to the corner where Steve sat. "Good drink," he said. "Wine. I make from blueberries."

"No, thank you," said Steve. Joseph looked puzzled, but he took the cup and went back to his friends.

While the men talked, Steve shared cookies with the children and practiced his Eskimo words on them. They thought it a great game and delighted in correcting him.

The evening wore on. The women and children went to bed in the other room, but Joseph's friends grew louder and louder. They must be telling jokes, Steve decided, judging from the way they laughed.

He zipped up his sleeping bag and tried to shut out the noise. Maybe it hadn't been such a good idea to come without Victor.

If I could speak Eskimo, the people would listen better, he thought. I'm going to go back to Koyalik and do some serious studying.

The room was too warm, and it smelled of fish, of seal oil, of unwashed men. Good thing he hadn't brought Liz. Steve took off one of his shirts and unzipped the sleeping bag.

I must have been mistaken about that boy, he thought drowsily. If he'd been interested, he would have stayed around afterwards . . .

A burst of laughter startled him awake, and he began thinking about Koyalik again. Had the Mission read his letter yet? What had they decided? . . . Maybe he and Liz could do more singing at the Sunday service. The Eskimos had liked that. He'd leave first thing in the morning so they'd have time to practice.

Joseph's party seemed to go on all night, but finally everyone went away. The next morning, sunlight awakened Steve from uneasy dreams, and he sat up with a jerk. It must be almost noon. Saturday noon! He had to get back to Koyalik by tonight.

Everyone in the cabin was still sleeping, but he hurriedly picked up his things. He went outside to pack the sled, and the dogs greeted him with noisy affection. They were ready to go too.

While he was straightening the harnesses, a man's voice spoke behind him. "Leaving us so soon?"

A lean, wiry Eskimo stood there, with the boy beside him. The man's face was weather-beaten, marked with the purplish-black scars of frostbite. He smiled and extended a hand. "I'm Ben Tignak. This is my son, Charlie."

"How do you do," Steve said, astonished.

Ben Tignak spoke again in perfect English. "Charlie tells me you were having a bit of a problem with your interpreter last night."

"I thought I was the problem," said Steve.

Ben Tignak stepped closer, his black eyes glinting with humor. "Joseph is a fine man, but when he's translating, he likes to make up words for the ones he doesn't know."

Steve smiled. "Well, that explains a lot."

The dogs moved restlessly. Bandit snarled at Howler, and Howler backed away. Steve put a hand on Bandit's collar. The boy's gaze seemed to follow his every move.

Joseph stepped out of the cabin and said something.

"It's a pleasure to meet you, Steve," said Ben Tignak. "Please excuse me." He gave his son a look that Steve couldn't interpret and went into the cabin with Joseph.

Steve glanced at his watch. If only they'd come earlier! But he had to leave, right away. He went on with harnessing the dogs, and the boy—Charlie—stood silently watching him.

"Look," said Steve as he finished up, "I'd really like to visit with you and your father. But I'm in a hurry to get back to Koyalik."

Charlie flicked a glance at the dogs and gave him a long, measuring look. "Better not go now."

"I'll come back, soon as—"

"Storm coming."

Not another one, Steve thought. What a country! He looked up at the mountains. They stood crisp and white against the blue sky. "Looks pretty clear."

"The dogs tell me. Storm coming," Charlie said firmly. "They know."

It was true; his dogs had been unusually restless this morning, Steve thought, but they were always eager to get going. Howler lifted his nose and whined. He wasn't acting much like a leader today.

Steve smiled at the boy. "I'm just going down the river a short way, and it's important for me to get back for Sunday. Please tell your father I'd like to talk to him again."

He waited, expecting the boy to say something more, but he didn't. Steve released the brake. The dogs plunged forward, almost jerking him off his feet.

After their first burst of energy wore off, Steve expected the dogs to run steadily, but they didn't. To his surprise, they seemed more and more reluctant to run at all. He glanced at the sky. It had grown overcast, but that wasn't unusual.

They haven't gone far enough to be tired, he thought. We haven't even reached the river yet. "*Gih,* Howler!"

A little wind arose, whispering threats, but he called to the dogs, telling them to hurry. They ran faster, slowed a little, then speeded up when Steve shouted at them again. Finally, Howler slowed in earnest, then he stopped, sniffing the air. His nose was covered with thick frost.

It had suddenly become much colder, Steve realized. And much too quiet.

Howler looked back at him and began digging a hole in the thin snow of the tundra.

The dogs know.

"Don't do that!" Steve leaped to grab Howler's collar. He tugged with all his might and finally turned the big husky around. Then he reached for Mikki. "Come on, boys; we're going back."

Slowly the dog team turned with their leader and headed back toward Shanaluk.

The wind gusted, bringing snow and a sudden whiteout. The air turned white. The horizon disappeared. Clouds and snow merged into a wall of grey nothingness and swallowed the dogs. Steve had to strain his eyes to keep track of them.

The team still ran, pushed across the tundra by the wind, but any moment now they would stop and burrow down, and then . . .

The wind cut through his fur parka like an icy blade and threw powdery snow in his face. His panting breaths rose in a frozen cloud of white.

How much farther? He wasn't even sure that they were going in the right direction.

A shout came, far ahead in the swirling white, and Howler swerved toward the sound. A man's voice, then a boy's high tenor called out. Somewhere just ahead of them was a dog team. His dogs surged forward, following it.

They ran on and on, and sometimes Steve lost sight of the other team. He hung onto the sled, letting his thoughts drift back to Koyalik. What was Liz doing today? Had this same storm hit them? What about the service on Sunday?

He glimpsed a darker blur in the blizzard of white and dragged his thoughts back to reality. He estimated the wind speed. He computed the wind-chill factor. Right now, the temperature must be . . . eighty below.

After a while, he could not think anymore. He had to concentrate on holding tightly to the sled. Feet numb. Hands numb. Hold on.

Now the sled was passing the dark outlines of cabins. A village. Both dog teams stopped. Steve shook himself awake. He stepped off the sled and fell sprawling into a snowdrift. For a minute he lay there, then reluctantly pushed himself up out of the tempting softness.

The dogs. He had to feed the dogs.

Someone took his arm, a short, snow-covered someone, and dragged him past the dogs into a cabin. The door closed behind them, and Steve leaned against a wall, trying to catch his breath.

"You stay," said a voice.

He tried to speak but discovered that his jaw muscles were frozen.

The person went back outside. Steve's knees buckled under him, and he slid down the wall. After a few moments he roused himself. He crawled closer to the stove, his face tingling with pain. Frostbite?

He awoke to warmth and more pain. Ben Tignak and an old woman were bent over him, doing something with his feet and hands and face. Then they made him drink something hot. He slept again.

The next time he awoke, no one was in the room, but a lantern glowed on the table. Outside, the wind still roared. The sound of it chilled Steve in spite of his sleeping bag. He sat up slowly.

This cabin was no larger than Joseph's, but it was cleaner and seemed more roomy. Shelves, hooks, and drying lines kept things off the floor. One long shelf was filled with books.

Ben Tignak came in, slamming the door behind him, his parka covered with snow. "Well, sir, it looks as if you decided to wake up and see the world," he said. He gazed at Steve with piercing black eyes.

"I'm afraid I've been a lot of trouble, Mr. Tignak," said Steve.

"Just call me Tignak."

Charlie stepped quickly into the cabin, carrying a block of frozen meat, and paused to look at him. "Charlie, I owe you an apology," Steve said. "You tried to warn me. And thank you both for coming after me."

Charlie said nothing. But he gave Steve a smile and went toward the stove.

"No problem," answered his father. "We've all learned from the dogs. Now let's get something to eat."

A shy little girl appeared from the back room, along with a woman who looked very old but served up a hot meal in no time. While they ate, Steve answered Tignak's questions about why he had come to Shanaluk, and he asked a few of his own. He found out that Tignak had learned his excellent English while he worked as a guide in Fairbanks and then as an army scout during the war.

"I'd give anything to be able to speak Eskimo as well as you do English," said Steve. Charlie looked astonished, but Steve went on, "I've got my little notebook and I'm collecting words, but I can't even put a sentence together yet."

"That's part of your problem," said Tignak. "Eskimo words are made up of stems and many different endings. The ending depends on how the word is being used in the sentence. That's hard to learn by yourself."

"I have trouble even writing down the words I hear." Steve shook his head, remembering. "Sometimes I wonder whether Eskimo uses the same alphabet we do."

"Same letters, yes, but the spelling is difficult. Eskimo has only three main vowel sounds—*a*, *i*, and *u*—" said Tignak. "And two sounds for the letter *k*."

They talked some more, and after they finished eating, Steve slept again. When he awoke, another meal was ready.

He and Tignak talked for a long time over bowls of steaming moose stew. Charlie listened quietly, but Steve felt the bright eyes studying him.

Steve learned how Tignak and his family had come to be living in Shanaluk. When Tignak married, he had followed Eskimo custom and moved to Shanaluk, his wife's village. Except for the disruption of World War II, they had lived in peace until a year ago, when his wife and two of his sons had died in a sickness that swept through the village.

"But I'll never go back to city life," said Tignak thoughtfully. "Too much noise; too many machines."

"No good hunting," said Charlie, as if that settled any doubt in his mind.

Steve thought about the difference between Chicago and Koyalik, and nodded in agreement.

"So," said Tignak, "what's next for you? If this storm ever blows past, we'll have to let you go back to your wife in Koyalik."

"Poor Liz!" exclaimed Steve. "I promised I'd be back for Sunday and—what day is this anyway?"

"Monday," said Tignak. "Monday evening, to be exact. But if it's any comfort, I think the weather will improve by tomorrow."

Tignak was right. Overnight the blizzard ended, and Steve got up at dawn to rouse the dogs from their snow burrows.

When he was ready to leave, he thanked Tignak and Charlie again for taking care of him and his dogs.

"You must come back soon." Tignak's black eyes sparkled. "My English has grown rusty, and I have many questions yet to ask." He shook Steve's hand in his courteous manner. As Steve drove off, Charlie lifted an arm in farewell.

The soft snow on the tundra slowed the dogs and made Steve wish he'd brought his snowshoes, but after several long hours, they finally reached the river. The wind-swept ice had only a thin layer of snow, and the sled seemed to fly the rest of the way to Koyalik.

They've had a blizzard here too, he thought as he drove into the village. Everyone was digging out, and several people waved as he mushed by.

The snow was piled in deep drifts around their little cabin, but someone had tramped down a narrow path to their door.

Liz ran out of the cabin while he was still unharnessing the dogs. "I'm so glad—so glad!" she exclaimed. She threw her arms around him. "I hoped you weren't caught in that storm."

"I sure have a story to tell you," he said.

"Oh, your face—it's got those patches of frost again! Here, let me help you with the dogs. Oh, Mikki, you look so good. Did the dogs fight, Steve?"

"Good old Bandit again. Kept snipping at Howler."

Once inside, Steve couldn't get warm until he'd built up the fire and stood over it for a while. Liz made coffee, then she served him a big plate of beans from the pot on the back of the stove.

She told him about the story time she'd had with five children while he was gone. He told her what had happened at Shanaluk and described Charlie and Tignak.

"I'm going to take you to meet them," he said. "You'll like Charlie."

"How old do you think he is?" asked Liz.

"Maybe fourteen, like your little brother. And he has the same look on his face."

"Like Danny?" Her face lit up. "The Great Investigator?"

"You said it. That boy watched every move I made. Looks smart too." Steve laughed. "He probably gets it from Tignak. I'm amazed at how well educated that man is. He's got at least one whole shelf of books—the most I've seen since we came to Alaska."

Slowly he finished the beans, thinking about the kindly interest in Tignak's dark eyes. "It's a wonderful thing the Lord has done. We've got an opening in that village now, and a good place to stay."

Liz put a plate of cookies beside him. "Perhaps more of an opening than we have here," she said gravely.

"I'm sorry! I really tried to get back for the service," he said. "Did anyone come?"

"No. But maybe it was the storm. I read some Scripture with Nida and prayed, but I'm not sure how much she understood."

"That's just it," said Steve. "We've got to learn the language. I hope Victor gets back soon."

The Mission must have received our letter by now, he thought. Had the plane come in on Monday? "Any mail?"

"Letters from my folks," Liz said. "Nothing from the Mission yet."

He pushed his chair back from the table and stood up, feeling suddenly exhausted. "Tomorrow I'll do some more visiting. And listening. Seems like the Trading Post is a good place to meet people. Maybe Gus will let me help him for a while."

Thursday morning, Steve was making some entries in his dictionary when the mail plane buzzed overhead on its way to the landing strip. It usually left immediately, and he waited to hear it take off again. But it didn't.

Maybe Jackson went up to the Trading Post, he thought. I ought to walk up there and see how he's doing.

He was putting on his parka when someone banged on the door. A young Eskimo boy stood there, panting. "Gus say you come quick."

10 Jackson

The boy took him to Gus's living quarters above the Trading Post. Gus was bent over someone on the sofa.

Jackson.

The pilot's eyes were closed, and his face was flushed with fever. The scar on the side of his head stood out, starkly white.

Gus looked at Steve. "Pneumonia," he said, his voice rough with worry. "The rascal's been flying around pretending to be immortal. Now he can't even stand up."

"There's no doctor?"

"The closest one is Nome. A hundred and fifty miles away. He needs a hospital too. They ought to tie him to a bed and pour some antibiotics down his throat. Might save his life."

Steve waited, hoping Gus would get to the point soon.

Jackson coughed, a harsh, rasping sound in the quiet room.

"Well?" said the trader.

Steve took his eyes from Jackson with an effort. "What can we do to help him?"

"We could fly him to Nome," said Gus.

"Fly him?"

The old man grabbed Steve's arm. "You're a pilot, aren't you?"

"But—"

"You came here to fly around Alaska and do good deeds, didn't you? There's a perfectly fine plane out there, and this man will die if we don't get him to a hospital."

Objections clicked through Steve's mind. *I've never flown in Alaska. I've never flown a plane on skis. I don't know the route to Nome.*

"Okay," he said. "Let's get going."

He hurried back to the cabin and told Liz what had happened, then asked her to make him some sandwiches and a Thermos of coffee. He packed his duffle bag with extra clothes and emergency gear and crunched through the snow to the airstrip.

Carefully he strained gasoline into the plane's gas tanks through a piece of chamois. Jackson always did it that way, so it must be important up here. Something about ice crystals in the fuel, he'd said.

While he did the preflight inspection, he prayed. "Lord, help me not to forget anything. Thank You that I've flown this kind of plane before and I'm still current in it. But what about the skis? Thank You for clear weather—if it stays clear . . . Lord, I need You!"

"What's taking you so long?" said Gus.

Steve looked up from checking the oil in the engine. "You want this plane to go down on the ice because I missed something? I'm almost done. You could get the passenger aboard—that's going to be a project."

He muttered reminders to himself as he walked around the tail of the airplane, studying the control surfaces. By the time he finished the preflight, they had removed the copilot's seat and put a makeshift stretcher in its place.

"Okay, Gus, hop in," said Steve. "We're ready to go."

Gus backed away from the plane. "I didn't say I was coming too."

"How do you suppose I'm going to find the airport in Nome?" asked Steve. "Or get Jackson to a hospital? I could waste a lot of valuable time figuring out what to do."

Gus thought for a moment. "I'll get Henry to go along with you." He turned and spoke to the Eskimo who had helped load Jackson onto the plane. Then he nodded. "Henry's flown up there a couple of times on the mail plane, and he'll make sure they take care of Jackson."

"Very thoughtful of you." Steve grinned to take the edge off his words. "We should get back tonight, if all goes well."

If all goes well. His stomach knotted as he climbed into the airplane and saw Jackson lying so quietly on the stretcher. But once he'd clamped on his seatbelt and adjusted the headphones, he relaxed in the seat. He'd done this a hundred times before.

As the engine warmed up, he set the gauges and studied a chart he had found under the seat. Beside him, Jackson stirred restlessly and coughed. Steve glanced over his shoulder. Henry sat calmly in the back seat and made no attempt to talk over the roar of the engine.

He eased the plane down the runway, thinking about the snow and those skis. It bumped alarmingly over the rough, icy surface, and he glanced at Jackson with concern. But then the jarring stopped, the airplane lifted, and he knew they were in the air.

He banked the plane in a long, smooth turn and headed up the coast toward Nome.

They flew north along the cliffs that rose at the ocean's edge. The shelf ice along the shore sparkled in the pale sunlight. Beyond it was the ice pack: rough, heaped-up, glistening piles of ice. Far in the distance lay the grey blue of open water.

That shelf ice might be flat enough for an emergency landing, Steve thought. But for now I'd rather not find out.

The snow-covered tundra stretched off to their right, looking deceptively smooth. Steve remembered the tussocks under that snow and hoped he'd never have to try a landing.

The plane's engine hummed steadily as the miles slipped past under their wings. Once in a while they flew over an Eskimo settlement. Each one looked like a handful of dark pebbles thrown down in the endless expanse of snow.

Steve was scanning the shelf ice when Henry touched his shoulder. The Eskimo pointed to a large cluster of buildings on the horizon.

No trees, no railroads—just a few houses huddled beside the frozen sea, thought Steve. But this must be Nome. He could hardly remember flying in on the big plane from Fairbanks.

Henry pointed again, at the blinking red light of a radio tower, and Steve nodded. He picked up his microphone. "Nome radio, this is mail flight 1355 Delta. I'm inbound southeast over the ocean. I'm landing at Nome; medical emergency onboard."

"Roger, 55 Delta; who is this? And what's the nature of your emergency?"

"I'm Steve Bailey, from Koyalik. Ah . . . I've got your friend Jackson on board; he's come down with something— might be pneumonia. Need to get him to a hospital fastest way."

"Understand, 55 Delta; we'll have transportation ready when you arrive."

The runway at Nome was in good condition, and after they landed, it took only a few minutes to see that Jackson was safely on his way to the hospital. They had to sit at the airport for a while, but finally one of the pilots had time to fly them back.

They landed at Koyalik as twilight faded into darkness. Steve climbed stiffly from the plane, waved to the pilot, and shook Henry's hand. "Many thanks—*Kuyana*—" he said.

Henry beamed and said something in swift Eskimo, then strode off into the village.

After Steve had talked briefly to Gus, he tramped back through the snow to his cabin, thinking about the day.

Three hundred miles! And the whole trip had taken less time than it did to mush the forty miles to Shanaluk.

That evening he and Liz prayed together, as usual. "Peter is right," he said. "I believed him before, but now I've experienced it and I'm really convinced."

Liz looked at him. "What . . . ?"

"I think we're going to need an airplane," said Steve. "Let's talk to the Lord about it."

The next day they saw Nida at the Trading Post, and she told them that Victor had returned. "He get caribou and much furs," she said. Her white teeth gleamed in a happy smile. "Come and see. Eat supper too."

Nida served a good meal, and Victor told story after story about his adventures. Then Steve described how he'd found Shanaluk.

Victor chuckled. "So you never get to Mierow Lake? Maybe we go sometime. First I hunt for *oogruk*. Tomorrow. Want to come?"

"Sure," said Steve. "We can take my team. I'd like to try Mikki as lead dog, but I'm afraid he's not big enough."

"He plenty strong," said Victor. "Smart. Most important question—do he have brave heart?"

Late that evening, Steve and Liz walked slowly back to their cabin under a sky filled with stars. "I've never seen the stars so brilliant," said Liz.

"Hmm," said Steve.

"What's the matter?"

"Well, I must admit, I'm disappointed," he said. "I was hoping Victor would be more interested in going to Mierow Lake with me."

Liz took his arm. "Not everyone in the world wants to get things done by yesterday."

Steve thought about that. "Victor's done a lot for us," he said at last. "And I know now that I'd be crazy to go alone. I guess I'll wait."

Liz was smiling at him.

"Yes, I *can* wait," he said, hoping that he could. "Meanwhile, there's the seal hunt tomorrow. Who knows . . ."

It was midmorning when they met outside Victor's cabin, but the winter sun was just rising. Steve's team would pull a sled loaded with Victor's kayak, a smaller sled, and the guns. Howler didn't seem to mind when Steve put Mikki in the lead position, and Bandit seemed good-natured for once.

"*Gih,* Mikki!" The young husky lunged into his harness, almost dragging the dog behind him off its feet. Steve smiled to himself.

The stormy tide had cracked the shelf ice that edged the beach. But the cracks were narrow enough to step across, and a light cover of snow made for easy sledding.

Two or three miles out from shore, traveling grew more difficult. The storm had broken up the deep-water ice pack and blown it back against the shelf ice with such force that ridges of broken and buckled ice had piled high. "We call these *eewoonucks*," said Victor.

They climbed over a twenty-foot ridge of clear green ice and slid down through the tumbled blocks on its other side. The second ridge was as blue as a summer sky. "Come from far north," Victor said. "Polar ice."

They detoured around a long drift of snow and climbed one more *eewoonuck*. Below, the ice pack had broken into ice floes that had black leads of open water between them.

Victor stopped to survey the ice. "Seal live here in winter," he said. "You stay with dogs. Point if you see one."

He took the kayak down to the edge of the ice and slipped it into the water. Then he paddled silently away, a tiny figure among the towering islands of ice.

Steve settled the dogs on a shelf of ice. They seemed to have accepted Mikki as their new leader. The team lay quietly, except for Bandit, who was chewing on his harness. He stopped when Steve spoke sharply to him, but he wore an injured air.

A rifle cracked, and before long, Victor returned with a small hair seal to load on the sled. Then he was gone again between the shifting floes.

Two of the dogs rose and stretched. Bandit stood up too. He arched his back and looked at Mikki. He pranced on his toes over to where Mikki lay.

As soon as Mikki sat up, Bandit leaped on him with a snarl. Mikki threw him off, and Bandit lunged at him again. The two rolled on the ice in a fury of teeth and fur and tangled lines.

Before Steve could get to his whip, the fight was over. Bandit lay on his back, and Mikki stood over him, growling.

Steve grabbed Mikki's collar and pulled him off the other dog. Good for you, he thought.

Bandit got slowly to his feet and staggered a short distance away. Steve checked his wounds. "Just a few nips, boy. Now you know who's boss. No more fighting, okay?"

Victor had been gone for a long time, it seemed. Steve climbed to the top of the *eewoonuck* to look for him. There he was, not far away; he'd been out of sight behind a tall ice floe.

Off to Steve's right, something moved. A large seal was pulling itself onto a pan of ice. Maybe it was an *oogruk,* the kind Victor wanted. He waved at Victor and pointed.

Victor turned his kayak and a few minutes later approached the seal from behind. It raised its head warily, then Victor's rifle snapped and it collapsed.

Victor climbed out of his kayak, up onto the ice pan to get the seal, and Steve began to worry.

That's an awfully small piece of ice, he thought. I just hope . . .

Victor eased the seal into his kayak, but as he straightened up, the ice pan tipped him into the water. He grabbed for the prow of his kayak and caught himself from going under.

Steve rushed down the icy ridge. Victor would freeze to death in minutes.

11   Mierow Lake

By the time Steve reached the water's edge, Victor had hauled himself back into his kayak and was paddling toward him—fast.

Quickly they loaded the seal onto the sled and lashed the kayak in place. Victor's breath came in short, painful gasps. He was wet, except for his oiled sealskin boots, and already his outer clothes were beginning to freeze.

It's twenty-five degrees below zero, Steve thought. How can he stand it?

"You go on ahead," he said to Victor. "I'll bring the dogs and the sled."

Victor grunted. Then he turned stiffly and soon disappeared over the nearest *eewoonuck*. Steve harnessed the dogs and followed more slowly.

The short winter day had almost ended, and the setting sun cast a glow of red across the ice.

At least, with the sun at my back I can keep going in the right direction, Steve thought.

Soon the sky grew dark and stars appeared. In the north, a flicker of green and yellow unfurled across the sky and became a shimmering banner.

No time to stop and watch, he thought. Besides, he was getting colder every minute. The icy chill of the tumbled green and blue ridges crept through his fur parka. Every time he stopped to untangle the dogs or lift the heavy sled around a hummock of ice, his hands grew more numb.

If I'm cold, he thought, *what must Victor be feeling? Lord, by Thy mercy, please keep him alive.*

Finally they reached the smoother shelf ice, and he called encouragement to Mikki. The whole team leaped ahead. Steve ran behind the sled, forcing his wooden legs to move. They had no feeling in them, and he tried not to think of stories he'd heard about frozen feet and hands.

Victor's uncle hurried out to meet them at the shore. "How's Victor?" asked Steve.

"Okay," said the man. "I take sled. You get warm."

"*Kuyana,*" said Steve, and he stumbled gratefully toward his cabin.

Liz was waiting with hot tea and questions about the trip. He told her how Victor had narrowly escaped freezing and how Mikki had established his place as team leader. Then he tried to describe the colors of the ice and the sunset and the Northern Lights.

"What a wonderful God we have," she murmured. "Merciful to you and Victor, and the one who created such beauty."

"I know what you mean," said Steve. "If only these people could understand what He's like . . . ." He paused. "That gives me an idea. For Sunday's message, I was going to preach about God, the mighty Creator. Telling them about the trip would make a good opening."

On Sunday, three families came to the meeting at Victor's house. There were several babies and young children who made the usual noises, but their mothers tended to them, and no one seemed distracted.

After his experience with the interpreter at Shanaluk, Steve was more thankful than ever for Victor. People nodded or smiled or looked serious in all the right places. Victor must be doing a good job.

Nida invited Steve and Liz to come back that evening. Liz baked a cake, and Steve brought along their notebooks, hoping to pick up some useful Eskimo phrases. After Tignak had told him about Eskimo stem words and endings, he'd made separate sections for word stems and endings, but he still found it hard to unscramble the long Eskimo words.

That evening, Victor told one hunting tale after another in his broken English. Then, to Steve's delight, he began talking about the trip to Mierow Lake as if it would be a great adventure.

"First thing, we ask Gus. He know where to go." Victor's eyes twinkled. "Don't want to get lost."

Steve grinned. "At least my dogs are smarter than I am."

"Your dogs good and strong now?" asked Victor. "Need to be strong this trip."

"Getting stronger every time I take them out. Now they last longer than I do."

"How about that *mik-shrok?*"

"Oh, Mikki? He's grown a lot. Of course, he gets special food." Steve smiled at Liz. "But he's worth it." Then Steve told Victor how he'd been trying out different leaders and how Mikki had won the fight with Bandit.

"That dog, he pull with heart," said Victor. "And he . . . what you call him? Smart cake?"

Liz giggled, then she put a hand over her mouth. Steve nodded. "Smart cookie. Yes, he sure is. I think I'll keep him as leader. The Lord sent us a good dog."

"Nida," Liz said suddenly, "we don't want to leave you here alone. Could you come too?"

Nida smiled and shook her head. Victor answered for her. "Nida take boys and go visit sister in Nome. She stay for a week or little bit longer. May be I bring her nice fox skin. May be we get a caribou." His eyes gleamed. "Gus say caribou run by Mierow Lake. We go soon; how about Wednesday?"

On Monday, Steve made sure he talked to each person who had ever come to a Sunday service or to Liz's story time. He tried to explain where they would be going and why they'd be away for a week or more.

That night he and Liz talked about the visits they had made. "I don't want them to think I'm just off on a hunting trip with Victor," he said. "But I'm not sure they understood me. I don't think any of them are true Christians, either."

"They're so friendly," said Liz. "They want to be nice, and they smile and agree with everything you say. The children are well behaved and amazingly polite. I wish we could figure out what they're really thinking."

"That's one reason we've got to learn Eskimo," said Steve. "Be sure to pack our notebooks. And by the way, do you know how to make bannock?"

"No," said Liz. "What's that?"

"A kind of crisp biscuit that's good to take on trips. You mix flour, lard, salt, baking powder, and water to make a stiff dough, then you fry it."

Steve consulted with Gus to make sure they'd be prepared for the worst weather.

"You and Victor will need to shoot some game along the way," said Gus. "But if you have to wait out a blizzard, you'll want something to keep you alive." He scratched the bald spot on top of his head. "Remember that the dogs will need plenty to eat. Most of the time they'll hunt on their own, but take along some dried salmon too."

Steve listened carefully, then he bought a small sturdy tent, a primus stove, some bales of dried salmon, and plenty of dried food such as beans and oatmeal.

When he packed the sled, he first spread out a heavy canvas tarp to line it. On the tarp he piled the bales of dried salmon and all their supplies. Then he pulled the tarp up and around and tied it snugly in place. On top, tucked under the ropes, went the ax, the guns, their snowshoes, and the big iron skillet.

He handed Liz a canvas bag. "We'll hang this below the handlebars."

"What's it for?"

"My hunting knife, the dog chains, maybe some extra rawhide. Better put in that extra waterproof match safe too."

"How about some chocolate and a few pieces of bannock?"

"Good idea!"

They left long before daybreak and drove for hours under bright moonlight. Steve felt as if they were traveling in another world—a frozen world of white and silver and shadowed black.

Liz rode on the sled for a long time, then she jumped off, saying she was cold. "I'll run with the dogs for a while," she said. "I'll tell Mikki to do me proud."

Victor must have heard her remark, for he called to Steve, "What's that—*do me proud?*"

"She wants Mikki to do such a good job that she'll be proud of him." He glanced at the dog. Mikki seemed to be pulling for the sheer joy of it, his floppy ear standing straight up in the wind. "So far, so good."

Victor grunted in agreement, and as they drove on, Steve heard him muttering, "So far, so good."

The first stretch of the river was familiar because of Steve's trips to Shanaluk. Later that morning, the sun rose slowly in a glow of pink, and in just a few hours, it began to set again. But they pushed on in the dusky light and finally reached Tall Rocks.

Huge icy boulders marked the fork of the river Gus had said to watch for. Behind the boulders rose the towering cliffs that had given the place its name.

Victor nodded toward the cliffs. "Rabbits in there."

They unloaded the sleds quickly and set up the tents. Then Steve and Victor grabbed their rifles. "I'll start a fire and get things ready," Liz said. "Good hunting!"

Back behind a clump of alders, Steve shot a snowshoe rabbit, and then Victor got one too. They crept through a snow-covered willow thicket and shot four more. "Dogs can hunt here too," said Victor.

After they returned to camp, Steve and Victor unharnessed the dogs and sent them to forage for their supper. One by one, the dogs came back to the fire, and Steve chained them close by. They curled up and watched the preparations for supper, looking contented.

The fragrance of wood smoke and sizzling meat reminded Steve of other winter camp-outs. But those trips had been just for fun—what a difference tonight!

He and Victor cut spruce boughs to use as cushions under the sleeping bags, and they all slept soundly.

On the second day, the river wound through a long rocky canyon, then opened out into a broad valley edged by mountains. When they stopped for the night, there were no sheltering rocks, but Victor knew what to do.

After the tents were up, he cut snow blocks and piled them around the base of each tent to keep out the wind. They didn't see any game, so they fried the rabbits they'd shot the night before and threw the bones to the dogs.

That night, Steve had hardly enough energy to feed the dogs and climb into his sleeping bag. If he was so tired, what must Liz be feeling? She hadn't said a word of complaint. But she'd been quick to accept the seal oil Victor offered for her windburned face. And she had fallen asleep before he blew out the candle.

For a long while he listened to an owl hooting deep in the forest. What would the people at Mierow Lake be like, he wondered. Lord, help me to tell them about You, somehow. And Victor needs You too . . .

After several hours of travel the next morning, they left the river at the pile of red-streaked rocks Gus had described and turned onto a dogsled trail. Gus had said the shortcut would save a whole day's travel.

The trail climbed up into the mountains through a forest of tall spruce trees. The grade was so steep that it was hard to keep the sleds upright, but the dogs pulled steadily onward.

Canada jays flitted through the trees, and chickadees called from every side. Liz pointed out the birds she knew and asked Victor about the others, but he wasn't sure of their English names.

Once Steve's team lurched forward in a sudden burst of speed, and the sled rocked dangerously on the narrow trail. Steve shouted to Mikki, and the dog slowed obediently to his usual trot.

Victor chuckled and pointed to tracks in the snow. "We cross rabbit trail. Dogs think it supper time."

By late afternoon they had climbed to the top of an especially high ridge, so they stopped for a rest. The sinking sun had turned the sky, clouds, and mountain peaks to gold. Below them spread a long valley, also touched with gold.

"Look!" exclaimed Liz. She waved at a flat, snow-covered expanse edged by rows of cabins. "Victor, do you think that's Mierow Lake?"

"Looks like." He grinned. "So far, so good."

The dogs must have sensed the end of the trip, for they raced down the mountainside, and Steve had to jump on both runners to keep the sled on the trail. As they drew closer to the village, he counted the cabins. More than either Shanaluk or Koyalik. Looked deserted, though. Where had everybody gone?

Halfway through the village, they saw an old woman carrying a bucket. Victor spoke to her briefly. "Caribou hunt," he told Steve. "Men come back tomorrow, may be."

"Ask her if there's any place we could stay," said Steve.

Victor discussed Steve's question with the woman for a long time. Steve caught a word here and there that he recognized, but he couldn't make sense of anything they said. An icy wind rose and seemed to blow right through him. The dogs drooped in their harnesses, waiting.

Finally, Victor turned back to them. "There is house at end of village. Nobody live there. Very old."

"I don't mind," said Steve, "as long as it has a roof and walls."

Victor spoke to his dogs, and they plodded slowly through the village. Steve's team followed to where a cabin stood close to the frozen lake.

More like a hut, Steve thought. It's plenty small. But it does have a roof.

The door hung off its hinges, and he pulled it open cautiously. Someone had once used the cabin for storage, judging by the dusty shelves and rows of nails in the log walls. The window had no glass in it. The dirt floor was littered with rubbish. And dogs had been kept in here.

Liz took a step backward. She looked up at Steve, and he put an arm around her. "It's just for a few days. We can clean it up."

Victor helped them shovel out the cabin, but he wouldn't sleep in it. He pitched his tent outside.

At bedtime that night, Steve whispered to Liz. "Victor's probably worried about *tungat*."

"So am I," she said. "The great big smelly ones that used to live in here."

"But even without a stove, it's warmer than a tent."

She nodded, yawned, and a minute later fell asleep. He lay awake for a while longer.

Cold air crept past the paper he had tacked over the window, and he pulled the sleeping bag more snugly around his shoulders.

God had brought them safely to Mierow Lake; he was thankful for that. But this wasn't the warm welcome he'd hoped for.

He didn't know these people, and it had been a long time since Peter was here. Would they even listen to his message?

I guess I'll just have to wait, he thought. Until tomorrow.

12 So Far, So Good

The hunters returned the next day in high spirits. They had shot several caribou, and everyone in the village would get a share. Perhaps no one would starve this winter.

After the feast that evening, Steve tried speaking to a group of the men. Most of them understood English, and they listened carefully.

He started by introducing himself and Liz and Victor. He told the men what had happened to Peter and how Peter had remembered them. They nodded and smiled, as if they remembered him too.

Then Steve showed them one of Liz's Bible storybooks and told the story of David as a young boy.

The pictures must have looked strange to them, Steve thought—all those people with white faces wearing brightly colored long clothes. And which of the Eskimos had ever seen a lion? But they leaned forward eagerly to see, and they exclaimed at the picture of David killing a bear.

Afterwards, Steve said to Liz, "This is so different from Koyalik. I can answer their questions by myself! I've been trying out a little Eskimo on them too, and they're helping me learn."

Steve preached twice on the second day, and he and Liz spent all their spare time visiting with the people. Steve had hoped that Victor would come with them, even though he wasn't needed to translate, but after a few visits, Victor grew restless. Finally, he went off in the afternoon and shot a caribou and a wolf, and he came back smiling.

The third day, the day they had to leave, came much too quickly.

One of the young men said, "The book with pictures. Maybe you let us have it a little while? Then you come back and get it?"

Steve glanced at Liz, and she nodded. Several of the young couples could read English. Perhaps they'd read the other stories and the Bible verses too, he thought. It would be a good reason to come back.

On their return trip to Koyalik, Steve realized that Mikki was no longer a thin, awkward puppy. He had put on muscle, and he pulled the heavy sled with surprising ease. He took orders like a dashing young soldier.

While they sat by the campfire that evening, Liz said, "Mikki's doing fine, isn't he? I've been watching the way he keeps the team in line. All he has to do is turn around and growl, and the bad guy straightens right up."

"You're right," said Steve. "When he's working hard, they do too. And when he decides to stop, they stop too."

Victor grinned. "And when he see rabbit, they all run with him."

"I'm afraid so," Steve said, shaking his head. That afternoon, a rabbit had dashed across the trail, right in front of Mikki, and he'd forgotten everything he ever learned. He had turned and raced after it, taking the whole team off the trail and into deep snow.

By the time Steve got the sled right-side up and the dogs untangled, they'd lost a whole hour of precious daylight.

"He learn," said Victor. "Never mind bad ear. Anytime you want to trade, I give you two dogs for that *mik-shrok*."

The second day of the trip, they shot rabbits for supper. After supper, Victor went hunting again. He came back with two Arctic foxes. "So far, so good!" he shouted, grinning broadly.

"Good for you!" Steve exclaimed. The rich white pelts were valuable, and Nida would be pleased.

They arrived in Koyalik just as a new storm blew in from the sea. They stopped at the Trading Post for the mail, then hurried home to unpack the sled and feed the dogs.

Steve built a roaring fire in the stove and split several armloads of wood to stack beside it. Then he hung their ice-rimmed parkas on the drying line he'd rigged near the stove. Liz hummed a tune as she warmed up some frozen caribou stew.

While they ate, they opened the letters that had arrived while they were gone. There wasn't anything from the Mission.

Liz finished reading her letter from home. "Mom's got big plans for . . . Steve! What's the date today?"

He glanced at the calendar on the wall. "Let's see. December. I think it's the fifth."

"We missed Thanksgiving!"

"We sure did. Well, we have a lot to be thankful for. I never thought we'd spend Thanksgiving at Mierow Lake."

"But I wanted to have a celebration," Liz said. "And invite everyone in the church and . . . " Her voice trailed off. "I wonder if they would have come."

"Why not? Oh, the *tungat* problem. Maybe they've forgotten about it by now."

Liz brightened. "You know what? We could have a feast at Christmas. That's coming up pretty soon."

"Sounds good to me." Steve glanced around the cabin, at the big, fur-covered bunk, the green-striped cushions Liz had made, the shelves he had built. He sighed in contentment. "It's good to be back, isn't it? *Tungat* and all."

Liz grinned at him. "So far, so good."

The storm meant that there'd be no mail on Thursday, of course, but Steve started on a letter for Peter right away. He'd want to know every detail of the trip to Mierow Lake. Then he wrote to the Mission, too, and told them about the new opening at Mierow Lake.

Liz wrote to their home churches and asked for special prayer about a ministry at Mierow Lake. That night, the wind howled around the cabin and beat at the windows until they rattled. Steve listened to the storm from the warmth of his sleeping bag and once again thanked God for bringing them safely home.

The next morning he found a miniature snowdrift inside the door. While they slept, a sifting of fine snow had come through the cracks in the door frame. He used scraps of fur to plug up every opening he could find.

On Saturday, the storm was still pounding the village, and Steve grew tired of pacing the floor and working on his indoor projects. He fought his way through the blizzard as far as the Trading Post.

A group of men that was larger than usual stood around the stove, and he joined them, wondering at their gloomy silence. Gus strolled past and took him back into the kitchen for coffee.

"Everyone looks so worried," Steve said. "What's the matter?"

"A man and his son got caught out on the ice in the storm," Gus said.

Something in his tone made Steve look up. "Still alive?"

Gus sighed. "The Eskimos don't think so. It's not impossible, but the family has given up hope—because of the boots."

"Boots?"

"They believe in signs from the spirits, Steve. The old shaman here told me about this. When a hunter is lost on the ice, the family hangs up his boots and watches for them to move. When the boots move a little, they say that the boots 'walk,' and it means the man is still alive. When the boots stop 'walking,' they say he will never wear them again."

Steve felt as if a heavy weight had fallen on his shoulders. I know they're pagans, he thought. So why does this bother me?

Gus poured himself another cup of coffee. "You look shocked."

"I didn't know there was a shaman in Koyalik."

"Used to be. He died. As a matter of fact, it's his cabin you're living in right now."

Steve took a gulp of the scalding coffee. "No wonder they're worried about the *tungat* in our cabin."

"Not surprised at all," said Gus. "Anyway, as soon as the storm lets up, everyone's going out to look for those hunters."

"I'm coming too."

That afternoon, the blinding snow lifted, and Steve joined the search party of dogsled teams. Since the weather was still bad and darkness was falling, they went in pairs.

Steve was paired with Henry, the Eskimo who had flown with him to Nome.

"Not good," said Henry, his face dark with sadness. "The boots, they do not walk anymore."

He scanned the shelf ice, and Steve tried to think of a good thing to say. The wind whipped past with a low, stinging hiss.

A thin film of snow sheeted across the ice and swirled at their feet. Then the wind rose higher, and conversation became impossible.

Henry waved out toward the pack ice, and Steve followed with his team.

For a long time they searched the *eewoonucks*.

They climbed the ridges of ice and peered into icy caverns until Steve's face stung and his hands lost all feeling. His voice grew hoarse from calling to Mikki against the wind.

A shout came over the ice, and they turned toward it. They found the other dog teams gathered nearby, in the shelter of a towering pile of ice. Men clustered around a sled that held two bodies.

Henry gazed at the sled. "This man just move to Koyalik last week." He stood silent for another minute, then slowly turned his dogs toward shore.

When Steve told Liz what had happened, she burst into tears. "These people live such a hard life, and they're dying right in front of us. Do you know who the hunters were?"

"No, they just moved here."

"But it could have been someone who comes to our services. Or someone from Shanaluk . . ."

She brushed the tears from her eyes and blew her nose. "It's been a long time since you went to Shanaluk. What about Tignak and Charlie? Do you think they've forgotten you?"

Steve put an arm around her. "Let's go see. First chance we get."

On Monday, the mail plane got through, and Jackson brought their mail down to the cabin himself. He handed Steve a bundle of letters and a package.

"Glad to see you looking better," said Steve. "Do you have time for a cup of something hot?" He put the handful of letters down on the trunk. Still nothing from the Mission.

"Sure do," said Jackson. "Thanks to you, I'm still alive and kicking. Yes, ma'am, coffee please. You make the best coffee around."

"I've got some blueberry pie here too," said Liz. "How's your appetite?"

"Food's starting to taste good again. And I'd never pass up a piece of your pie." Jackson sat down at the table and smiled at them both. "So what've you youngsters been up to lately?"

Steve described the trip to Mierow Lake and their plans for going back to Shanaluk.

Jackson nodded. "Pete told me about that village on Mierow Lake. He was so excited, you'd think he'd found the North Pole. Wish I could stick some stamps on you and fly you back there on the mail plane."

He paused to scrape blueberry sauce off his plate. "The guys at Nome said you made a nice smooth landing, Steve. It's fun flying on skis, isn't it?" His blue eyes twinkled. "Too bad I couldn't have been more help, but I guess I just wasn't paying attention."

He glanced at his watch and stood up. "I don't think you'll be going anywhere for the next few days, though. There's a bad weather system coming down the coast, heading right for Koyalik. I'd better get my bird out of here. Thank you for your kind hospitality."

After Jackson left, Steve opened the package. "The Bibles from Peter!" exclaimed Liz.

Steve gazed at the five sturdy red-covered Bibles for a minute, then he stacked them carefully on a shelf. "I'm going to pray that God will provide us with four men who will want these Bibles," he said. "Four Eskimos who will come to know Him as Savior and love Him with all their hearts."

"Four?" asked Liz. "Who's the other one for?"

Steve touched the Bible on the bottom of the stack. "That one's for Jackson. Someday, when the time is right."

A new storm swept into Koyalik that night. Between the bad weather, Liz's story time, and the Sunday service, a week passed before they could leave for Shanaluk.

They made good time and arrived late in the afternoon. Tignak's cabin was dark. Of course, he and Charlie could be away hunting, or they might be visiting in another cabin, Steve thought. But what about the grandmother and the little girl?

He hesitated, wondering whether to wait outside in the cold or go somewhere else.

Charlie backed slowly out of the cabin and closed the door. He stood there a moment, his young shoulders drooping, then he swung around and saw them.

He nodded in recognition.

Steve left the dogs and hurried across the snow toward him.

The boy waited, his face expressionless. "My father sick. I go to get the shaman."

He turned and started around the corner of the cabin.

"No, wait, Charlie," said Steve. "Maybe we can help."

The boy stopped. "Nothing help." His eyes were despairing. "I think he die."

13 Good Medicine

Tignak lay unconscious on a cot near the stove, covered with caribou skins. The lines on his face seemed to be etched in dark leather. His breath came in ragged gasps.

The room was warm, much too warm, Steve thought. He looked at Liz. "Good thing you took some medical training."

"That one-week course for missionaries? This isn't malaria." Liz pulled off her mittens and felt Tignak's forehead. "But I've nursed enough sick children to know a fever when I see it."

"He say he so cold; he shiver," said Charlie. "So I make a big fire—"

"You did fine," said Liz. "Now we need to make him a little cooler." She glanced at Steve. "I need some water and a clean cloth. And we have to get the skins off him, right away."

Tignak stirred and groaned when they lifted off the heavy furs. "Just one light sheet," said Liz. "Do you have any sheets, Charlie?"

"Yes, my sister, she like." He rushed into the back room, and Steve wondered again where the little girl and the grandmother had gone.

Tignak lay quietly as Liz bathed his face and arms with water. "That's better," said Liz, smoothing the hair back from his forehead. "Now he needs something to drink."

"We got lotsa tea," said Charlie.

"No, plain water is best." She gave him a sharp look. "Very clean water. Boil it for me, okay? Lots of it."

"I melt some ice." He hurried to boil the water, glancing up at Liz from time to time.

"Okay," she said. "Just take the pot outside for a minute to cool it."

As soon as Charlie brought the water back inside, she poured some into a clean cup. "Now talk to your father," she told Charlie. "Wake him up. He has to drink this."

Tignak mumbled without opening his eyes, but he drank from the cup that Charlie held to his lips.

Liz frowned. "I wonder how we could get him to take some aspirin." She pulled out their first-aid kit.

"My mother used to crush it and mix it with honey," said Steve.

"Charlie, do you have any honey? No? What about some sugar?"

Liz mixed aspirin and sugar with water to make a thin paste, and Charlie persuaded his father to swallow it.

Tignak frowned and made a face. He licked his lips, then he said something in Eskimo.

"He thirsty." Charlie leaped for the cup of water and held it for him to drink.

Charlie stepped back when the cup was empty, and Liz put a hand on his shoulder. "Good for you. We can let him sleep now. What in the world happened to him?"

"He take my grandmother and sister to visit in Fairbanks. When he come back, he si-i-ick." Charlie drew out the word for emphasis. "He hot and cold. He hurt all over in his bones."

"Sounds like he caught the flu," said Liz. "I've heard that it can be pretty serious up here."

"How long has he been sick?" asked Steve.

"Two—three days. I didn't want to ask shaman. My father not like. But he get worse and worse."

"I don't blame you for being worried," said Liz. "Your father is a very sick man. Can you get me a piece of caribou? I'm going to make him some good strong soup."

Steve and Charlie sat by Tignak's side while Liz worked on the soup.

"Tell me about your shaman," said Steve.

Charlie leaned forward, his dark eyes lively with enthusiasm. "He strong. He make sick people better. He warn us about bad spirits—tungat. Sometimes he go to spirit world and talk to them."

Tignak stirred, opening his eyes. "Mumbo jumbo," he said clearly. He closed his eyes again.

Charlie scowled and got to his feet. "I get more wood."

"I'll help you," said Steve.

He and Charlie went outside and carried armloads of wood into the small entry room. They piled it high, and then Charlie paused, his breath coming in frosty clouds. "Our shaman, Am-nok, he do wonderful things. Not so much anymore. Maybe he getting tired."

"Have you ever seen him heal anyone?" asked Steve.

Charlie nodded. "A sick man with pains in his stomach. Am-nok talk to man. He have a drum, and he talk to spirits. The whole family come to watch. Am-nok sing all night, put oil and food in the fire. When morning come, man all better."

He didn't look at Steve or wait for a comment. He kicked the snow off his boots and went back into the cabin. Steve followed.

From the stove, Liz looked up at them with a smile. "Soup's ready," she said.

As soon as Charlie had taken off his parka, she handed him a cup of steaming liquid. "See if you can get your father to drink a little bit."

Charlie gazed suspiciously at the brown liquid. "What this?"

"Caribou tea." She sent Steve a glance. "The Arctic version of beef broth."

While Charlie spooned up the tea for Tignak, Steve paced back and forth in the small room. With Tignak so sick, there'd be no preaching on this trip. He didn't want to take a chance on using Joseph for an interpreter again.

He sighed in exasperation. At least tomorrow he could go see how Joseph and his family were doing.

The next morning Tignak was strong enough to talk and handle a cup on his own. "Good medicine," he said to Liz. "I'm grateful to you." His dark eyes had regained their brightness.

Liz put away the dish she had been wiping and sat down next to him. "I've been snooping in your library." She waved a hand at the long shelf of books over their heads. "Tell me how come you're reading some of my favorite books? There's poems by Robert Frost; plays by Shakespeare . . ."

"Easy," said Tignak. "I worked as a guide for a doctor in Fairbanks. He taught me English, and whenever we were in town, he'd let me read books from his library. When we were out on the trail, he'd quote poetry by the hour. After a while I decided to buy some books of my own." He smiled. "Now, I guess I'd rather read a good book than do just about anything."

"What about Charlie?" asked Liz.

A shadow crossed Tignak's face. "Maybe someday. Right now he doesn't have his father's taste for books. He'd rather be out hunting."

The door banged open, and Charlie carried in a load of wood. "Mr. Bailey, I like your dog—the one who look like a wolf."

"Oh, Mikki?" Steve went over to help Charlie stack wood beside the stove. "Please call me Steve. Yes, he's doing very well."

"He look like a sma-a-a-rt dog."

"We hope so," said Steve. "Actually, he's my wife's dog."

Charlie looked at Liz with new respect. "Your wife?"

"Yes, she picked him out herself and paid for him with her own money."

"Charlie's become our family expert on dogs," said Tignak. "He's in charge of our team and does a good job of driving them."

"Do you take them hunting, Charlie?" asked Liz.

"Yes. Joseph is best hunter around. He help me train them."

"That reminds me," said Steve. "I was thinking of visiting Joseph today. I think he'd like to meet you, Liz."

"I saw him working by cabin," said Charlie. "I take you over there."

Joseph was still outside his cabin, and he was talking to an older Eskimo. At the sight of them Charlie hung back, but Joseph looked up with a smile.

Charlie stepped forward shyly, casting a sidelong glance at the old man. The boy spoke to Joseph in rapid Eskimo, and Joseph nodded.

"My good friend, Steve," he said. "I no see you long time."

Steve shook his hand. "I am glad to come back," he said. "This is my wife, Liz."

Joseph smiled again and introduced his companion. "This is Am-nok."

Steve made sure his smile did not change.

In broken English, Joseph went on to tell the shaman where Steve lived and how they had met.

Am-nok was not tall, but he had broad shoulders, and once he had been powerfully built, Steve thought.

The shaman's face was plump, crisscrossed with wrinkles, and his eyes were lost in slits of flesh. His boots— *mukluks*—were trimmed with yarn tassels and elegantly beaded, but otherwise he was dressed in furs like Joseph.

"Nice," Am-nok said, nodding to Steve. "Nice-to-have-you-here." His voice was high and thin. He bowed to Liz. "Nice-to-meet-you."

He gave them both a polite smile, then turned back to Joseph and began a long speech in Eskimo.

Charlie stepped back abruptly. "Time to go," he said. Neither Am-nok nor Joseph seemed to notice when they left.

While Charlie trudged ahead of them through the snow, Steve said, "Well, what did you think?"

Liz shrugged. "Joseph looks like your average Eskimo. And that nice old man seems harmless."

Steve grinned. "That nice old man is the village shaman."

"Hmm," said Liz. "I wondered what was the matter with Charlie."

14 Faster, Mikki!

The next morning, Tignak was definitely feeling better, and Steve decided that they should start back to Koyalik.

After they'd said good-bye to Tignak, Charlie followed them outside and helped to harness the dogs. When they were ready to go, Charlie stepped up beside Liz.

"You come back?" He glanced at her and then at Steve, his dark eyes hopeful. "I wait for you . . ." He paused, obviously struggling to find the right English word. "I wait for you with all my heart."

Liz put a hand on the boy's arm as if she did not want to let him go.

"We'll come back," Steve said. "You can count on it, Charlie."

At their first rest stop, Liz sipped her coffee in unaccustomed silence. Finally, she said, "What a kid."

"Who? Oh, Charlie."

"You're right; he's like Danny," she said slowly, "but he acts older in some ways."

"I guess kids grow up faster out here."

Liz nodded. "We've got to keep praying for him and Tignak." She smiled. "We've hardly left, and I can't wait to go back."

"Me too," said Steve.

He cupped the empty mug in his hand. "Lord, watch over them," he prayed silently. "I don't like the look of that Am-nok. Medicine man or shaman or whatever they call him—he's going to make trouble for Your work."

He spoke to the dogs and walked stiffly to the sled.

The day after they returned to Koyalik, Liz began baking cookies with an energy that surprised Steve.

He paused as he was putting on his *mukluks*. "Company coming?"

"Well, not for sure. But you know, we talked about Christmas, and I suddenly realized that it's next week. I'd love to invite everyone over for a feast."

Steve wondered about the *tungat* problem. But why discourage her? "I'd better get out and kill a seal," he said. "That's what they do around here, it seems. Or even a caribou. We could feed the whole village." He fastened his parka. "Seriously, though, we could have a special service. Then they could come here to eat if you'd like. Let's ask Victor and Nida what they think. I'm going up to the Trading Post to see if there's any mail."

During the past weeks they had received several very encouraging letters from their churches and friends, but still nothing from the Mission.

Steve prayed as he shuffled through the snow. "Lord, if that letter comes today, help me to accept their decision from Your hand."

His chest tightened when Gus handed him the distinctive grey envelope. He made himself carry it all the way back to the cabin without opening it.

"Back so soon?" Liz looked up from the stove. "Oh, from the Mission?" She put down the spoon she was holding. "Open it quickly, Steve, please."

He read it aloud. Good news. The Mission said they had been approved to work at Koyalik for a year; then the committee would meet again and discuss the situation.

Thank you, Lord! He looked at Liz. "The Lord knew we needed this encouragement."

"He knows! He's so good to us!" She ran to hug him, then turned back to the stove, still smiling. "You know what? The Mission hasn't had time to get your letter about Mierow Lake yet."

"That's right. By the way, I think we ought to pray about going back there soon."

"Okay, but not until after Christmas."

That night they talked to Victor and Nida about the idea of a Christmas celebration.

Victor looked at Nida, and Steve wondered what he was thinking.

"Good to have special service," she said brightly. "This time of year, we have festival. Lots of games, races. Lots of food."

"Great!" exclaimed Liz. "It sounds like fun. I hope Gus still has plenty of flour and raisins."

She baked a raisin cake and all of Steve's favorite Christmas cookies, and Steve chopped wood to meet the endless demands of the stove. He carried each package of cookies outside and stored it in their cache hut.

"Nice to have a freezer with unlimited space," he said.

He paused outside the cache. Our cache hut seems larger than most of the others, he thought. I wonder if they gave that old shaman a lot of food in payment for his work.

Steve and Liz made a point of visiting all the cabins in the village. Steve invited each family to the Christmas service, and Liz gave a special invitation to the children.

The mail plane arrived on the morning of Christmas Eve, but Jackson couldn't stay. "Got bad weather chasing me."

Sure enough, that night a series of storms moved in that postponed any Christmas celebration for a week.

Steve paced the floor in the little cabin, studied his word list, and brought Mikki inside so they could teach him some tricks. He and Liz made jokes about their absent Christmas gifts and tried to imagine where in snowbound Alaska the mail might be stranded.

One afternoon Steve wondered why the cabin was so dim, then he realized that snow had drifted halfway up their west window. The next morning, the whole west end of the cabin was buried in snow.

Every few days, Steve fought his way through the drifts to the Trading Post. Most of the Eskimos stayed at home during the storms, though, and he did too.

He finished building another set of shelves so Liz could unpack her precious books. She found her volume of Robert Frost's poems, and they read to each other from it. They prayed for Tignak and Charlie and wondered whether their cabin was half-buried in snow too. They started memorizing the book of Ephesians. They prayed about the Mierow Lake trip and the Christmas service.

"Only it's way past Christmas," Liz said. "We'll have to call it a New Year's service."

On Thursday, the mail plane made it through with much-needed supplies for the village and their Christmas packages from the States. And finally, the first Sunday in January, they held the special service.

Many people crowded into Victor's cabin, more than Steve had ever preached to before. There was a great deal of shuffling and crying of babies, but no one seemed to notice.

He spoke about Christ, God's gift to the world, and tried to make it short but meaningful.

What was Victor thinking as he translated? Steve wondered. He had talked to Victor about Christ, but the young Eskimo always smiled politely and changed the subject.

After they had sung a hymn, Steve invited everyone to come to their cabin for something to eat. Then he and Liz hurried off to make sure they'd be ready.

He built a roaring fire in the stove. Besides coffee and tea, Liz made two big pots of cocoa. They set out the cookies and sliced the raisin cake. Then they waited. Steve looked out the window again and again, but no one was walking down the path to their cabin.

Liz stood by the stove, twisting a dishtowel in her hands. Finally she said, "They aren't coming, are they?"

"Doesn't look like it, Lizzie." Steve sat down on the trunk. "The *tungat,* I guess. When Gus told me this used to be an old shaman's cabin, I had no idea these people were so afraid of the spirits."

Liz wiped her eyes with the dishtowel and hung it up. "Let's take some cake to Victor and Nida."

When they trudged over to Victor's cabin, they found it full of people. Everyone greeted Steve and Liz kindly.

Nida hurried to get them hot coffee. "Sit down, you two!" She pointed proudly to a shiny plastic table and chairs. "Brand-new. Just unpacked tonight for party. We get from States in catalog."

"Hello, hello!" said a woman. "Here, eat *muktuk.*" Another woman brought them plates heaped with vegetables and roasted caribou.

The men gathered to tell hunting stories, and Steve found that he could understand a few words and phrases. While he listened, he thought about the fears that these people hid behind their smiling faces.

It was late when they left Victor's cabin. "Well, Lizzie, there's your Northern Lights," said Steve.

The sky was swept by frosty white beams and arcs of light. Their small cabin stood like a black silhouette against the streaks of brightness that raced across the horizon.

"It's a good cabin the Lord gave us," Liz said suddenly. "And if there are any evil spirits around, He has certainly protected us from them."

"But, see, the people here don't know Him," said Steve. "And since we're white, it doesn't count that the spirits don't bother us."

"Even Victor and Nida don't visit us." Liz shook her head. "All the time we've been here. All the preaching they've heard. You'd think it would make a difference."

"It will, someday," Steve said. "C'mon. Let's finish packing for Mierow Lake."

In spite of his cheerful words, Steve felt as if he'd somehow failed. But he set his mind on making sure they had all they'd need for the trip. Victor wouldn't be going along—he had some trapping to do—so they were on their own.

They left early, as Steve had planned, and the first day went smoothly. As usual, Mikki threw all his energy into leading the team, and even Bandit behaved himself.

They camped near Tall Rocks, as before, and Steve shot rabbits for their supper. "Look at Mikki," said Liz. The dog held a ptarmigan in his mouth, quite frozen. "He must have grabbed it as he ran along the trail!"

As soon as he was unharnessed, Mikki sat down to eat his catch.

At the end of the second day, they stopped early so Steve would have time to cut snow blocks and set up camp properly. They could probably make up the extra hours tomorrow, he thought.

On the third day, Steve had trouble finding the right place to leave the river. "Red-streaked rocks," he muttered as the team trotted slowly on. There were plenty of rock outcroppings along the river, but they were covered with fresh snow.

Finally he turned the dogs and went back, stopping at each bank of rocks that might be high enough, until at last he found the trail.

"Now hurry," he said to Mikki. "We've wasted a lot of time."

He glanced at the western sky. The sun was beginning to set, but there would be light for a while. The snow was so deep that the dogs had trouble getting through it. Liz drove the team, and Steve went in front, wearing his snowshoes. By stamping down hard at every step, he broke a trail through the snow.

Even so, the sled tipped over twice on the steep slope, and they had to stop more times than Steve would have liked.

Finally, they reached a spruce forest, and under the tall old trees, the snow wasn't as deep. Steve began to hope that they could make up for lost time.

The wind sighed in the branches overhead, and a few snowflakes spun daintily past. He glanced up in alarm. The sky was stone grey and darkening.

"Faster, Mikki! Let's go, boy!"

Mikki leaned into his harness and set a new, faster pace. The team climbed one ridge after another, and then the dogs began to tire. They came out of the forest onto a wide slope that Steve thought he recognized, but it was drifted with soft, deep snow.

Mikki didn't falter. He plunged into snow up to his chest and fought his way through the drifts. The dogs floundered along behind him. Once again, Steve went in front of the team to tramp down a path.

Apparently no one has used the trail since we were here, he thought. Too bad there aren't any markers.

The wind was rising now, throwing handfuls of snow into their faces. He turned the team away from the deep snow, toward the trees at the top of the ridge, hoping for some cover. As long as they kept going in the same general direction, they wouldn't get lost.

Snow fell more heavily as they climbed the steep hillside, but Steve didn't want to stop. This was probably the ridge that overlooked Mierow Lake. If they could just get down the other side . . .

Liz had been following the sled on her snowshoes. Now she looked so tired that he told her to stand on the runners, even though it would add to the dogs' load. They kept on.

Near the top of the ridge they passed a few scattered trees, and then a wall of spruces loomed ahead. Their boughs hung so low that there was barely room for the dogs to pass under.

Abruptly Mikki stopped, tangling the whole team behind him. "*Gih*, Mikki!" shouted Steve. He'd never camped out in a blizzard, and he didn't intend to now—

Mikki lifted his head and howled. It was the long wolf-cry of the wilds, and it lifted the hairs on back of Steve's neck.

He peered through the blinding snow. "Mikki! Get going, boy! We're almost there."

Mikki answered with another wild howl.

The dogs dropped in their tracks. Steve snatched his whip and stumbled up the line to where Mikki stood.

He'd never beaten his lead dog, but he would now—if it would get the team moving.

"Mikki!"

The dog looked up at him and whined deep in his throat.

An icy warning halted Steve's upraised arm. *The dogs know.*

He dropped the whip and unharnessed Mikki, but roughly. Okay. They'd have to make camp here.

15 Mush Those Dogs

Liz was still clinging to the handlebars of the sled. She must be almost frozen. He put an arm around her and spoke gently to her, but she did not answer.

He hurried to untie the ropes on the sled, and she staggered over to help, moving slowly, as if in a stupor.

It took a long time to unharness the dogs, feed them, and set up the tent. The snow was too soft and loose to cut into blocks, so Steve tipped the sled on its side, hoping for some added protection from the wind.

His hands shook and he dropped the matches twice, but finally he got the stove going. Liz crouched over its feeble warmth with a sigh.

They melted snow for hot drinks and ate the rest of the bannock in the wavering light of a candle. Then they crawled fully dressed and shivering into their sleeping bags.

Snow whispered insistently against the tent walls, and the trees beside them creaked and groaned. Steve wished he'd had time to cut spruce branches for a mattress. It would've been a lot more comfortable than sleeping on the snow.

Every once in a while, the wind gusted and icy particles sifted through the tent walls.

We'll be snowed under by morning, Steve thought.

After a long time, Liz stopped shivering and seemed to fall asleep. Steve listened for a change in the sound of the wind. He wondered how far they were from Mierow Lake.

He slid deeper into his sleeping bag and tried to rest, but he could not.

This blizzard could last for days, he thought. We don't have a lot of food, and Liz . . .

He remembered how exhausted she'd been when they stopped. She hadn't said a word of complaint; she never did. But could she stand three or four more days of this bitter cold?

"Lord, what have I done wrong?" he whispered.

A dark shadow that he could not name fell across him. The work at Koyalik was going nowhere. Even Victor, who had listened to all his sermons, seemed unmoved. The group at Mierow Lake had been interested, but he could see now that a trip like this was too dangerous to attempt during the Arctic winter.

Maybe they shouldn't have asked to stay in Alaska. Maybe . . .

Have not I commanded thee? The verse flashed into his mind, bright as a flaming match. Steve drew a sudden breath.

Have not I commanded thee? The words flared higher, warm and comforting.

"Forgive me, Lord," he whispered. "Your timing is perfect. I will trust You to keep us safe. I will wait for Your time to bless these people. You're in command. *You.*"

As the night wore on, he grew colder and colder, but contentment glowed steadily inside him. Liz awoke, shivering again, and they whispered together in the icy darkness.

Liz spoke of Shanaluk. She reminded him of the opening there, of Tignak's kindness, and of Charlie's many questions. They prayed again for Tignak and Charlie.

Once again, they drifted off to sleep.

The wind fell silent just before dawn. As soon as the first grey light filtered into the tent, Steve tickled Liz out of her drowsy silence. "Storm's over, Lizzie. Let's get going."

They made tea and ate hot oatmeal, and then Steve ventured outside.

The snow lay thick over everything, and four of the dogs were still invisible in their snow burrows. Steve set to work shaking out the tangled lines, and the dogs poked their noses out of the snow. They greeted him with hungry, yelping cries.

Mikki was already up. Judging from his tracks, he had made several large circles around the tent; now he stood near the line of trees just beyond the tent.

Something about his silent waiting made Steve wonder what was the matter. He put down the harness and tramped toward him through the snow. The dog's tail hung low, and he looked worried.

Steve glanced past him, under the low spruce boughs, and stopped so fast he almost fell. Beyond the trees there was nothing. He inched forward and looked over the edge of a cliff. Far below lay a deep ravine.

"Mikki," he whispered.

A cold nose pushed up against his face.

"Mikki, if you hadn't stopped . . ." He put an arm around the dog's shaggy neck and drew him close.

Lord, how did he know it was there? Thank You for saving our lives.

Liz was still sitting in the tent looking dazed, but Steve dragged her out to see what he'd found. She hugged Mikki and talked to him until he pranced happily in the snow. Then, with renewed energy, they packed up the sled and set off.

Steve turned the dogs back in the direction from which they had come the night before. In the glow of sunrise he found the trail up the last high ridge, and they climbed it slowly.

By the time they reached Mierow Lake, it was midday. Two Eskimos hurried out of a cabin to greet them, and Steve recognized one of them as the man who had asked to borrow Liz's book.

"You come back!" he exclaimed. *"In the beginning, God created the heaven and the earth."*

Steve looked at him in amazement. "How'd you learn that?"

"In your book. We read stories. We learn Bible verses. See who says verses best. I win." He grinned broadly. "We wait for you. Come and see."

He led them to the cabin beside the lake. Someone had cleaned it out and put glass in the window. It had a stove now, and a homemade table with two chairs.

"This is wonderful! Thank you!" Steve glanced at Liz. Her face was shining.

A crowd of people had gathered, and everyone had something to tell them. Some unharnessed the dogs. Others helped to carry things inside the cabin.

They stayed for three days. Steve preached in English twice a day, and each time his listeners stayed afterward to talk and ask questions.

Liz met with a group of the women and told Bible stories to the children. Many adults came for the story time too.

Finally their store of supplies grew low, and Steve knew it was time to leave.

Reluctantly he packed the sled, and they said their farewells. Again and again he told the people, "Pray that God will bring us back."

The dog team started with a jerk, someone shouted a last good-bye, and they set off up the trail.

At the crest of the first ridge, they paused to look back at the cabins, small and dark in the frozen wilderness.

"I could have stayed there for weeks," said Steve. "Or even months."

Liz nodded. "The Lord is opening their hearts."

"He really is," said Steve. "They need a lot of teaching, though. It's going to take a while."

Liz gave him a mischievous grin. "How can you stand it?"

"Well, I'm trying to learn," he said, and he smiled.

Liz seized his arm. "C'mon, let's get going. Mush those dogs!"

"What's your hurry?"

"Charlie's waiting."